Are you an armchair dete

lover of history for whon ... ıs

outcome? If so, **The Wul**

The Wulf Enigma is an ambitious and accomplished work – fresh, fascinating and thoroughly enjoyable. – *Pansy Maurer-Alvarez*

This is a story to read and ponder a while, and then re-read, because it is so different to anything you will have read before, by Mandy Pannett or anyone else… a riddle, a poem, a quest.

– *Catherine Edmunds*

The Wulf Enigma is a beautiful novella that enacts its own theoretical position(s) about writing. It's as though John Fowles had become a poet and written a novella. I don't say this simply because Pannett's poetry appears within the novella but because of a compact vision that fills the pages. The writer understands that a novella is not a short novel but its own medium, one that can work with the compression of poetry against the dilation of prose. This novella asks really big questions: what makes an historical novel? How do we create characters? What is the difference between poetry and prose? And yet it does so with a lightness of touch and is never less than entertaining. This is a text I'll return to and which will continue, I am sure, to give me joy. – *Caron Freeborn*

We are creatures of memory and imagination. Remember that glimpse of someone or something waiting, beside you, behind you, gone? In just this way, figures in **The Wulf Enigma** will step for a moment out of the shadows, tease you with riddles, clues, questions, leave you with an imprint of themselves and their times, even as they vanish.

Copyright information

ISBN 9781910841-53-2

Printed in the UK
by Catford Print

Published by
Circaidy Gregory Press
Creative Media Centre,
45 Robertson St, Hastings,
Sussex TN34 1HL

www.circaidygregory.co.uk

The Wulf Enigma

by

Mandy Pannett

To Diane,

Very best wishes to you.

Mandy

Circaidy Gregory Press

Mandy Pannett

Dedication

Special thanks for everything to the wonderful
Green Room Poets: Judith Cair, Celia Dixie, Penny Hope,
Andie Lewenstein, Margaret Wilmot

Acknowledgements

A version of Part I of *The Wulf Enigma* was first published in 2016 in the journal *Snow*, edited by Ian Brinton and Anthony Barnett.

Some of the author's own poems in *The Wulf Enigma* have appeared in publications by **Sentinel Poetry Movement**, **Indigo Dreams Press** and **Oversteps Books**

Frontispiece

Text of Saxon poem commonly known as

Wulf and Eadwacer

Leodum is minum swylce him mon lác gife:
willað hy hine aþecgan gif he on þreat cymeð.
Ungelic is us.
Wulf is on iege, ic on oþerre;
fæst is þæt eglond, fenne biworpen;
sindon wælreowe weras þær on ige:
willað hy hine aþecgan gif he on þreat cymeð.
Ungelice is us.
Wulfes ic mines wid-lastum wenum dogode:
þonne hit wæs renig weder, ond ic reotugu sæt,
þonne mec se beaducafa bogum bilegde;
wæs me wyn to þon, wæs me hwæþre eac lað.
Wulf, min Wulf, wena me þine
seoce gedydon, þine seldcymas,
murnende mód— nales meteliste.
Gehyrest þu, Eadwacer? Uncerne earne hwelp
bireð Wulf to wuda.
þæt mon eaþe tosliteð þætte næfre gesomnad wæs
uncer giedd geador.

PART I

I'll begin with a quest. A quest for truth – or if that is impossible then a search for clues. I'll be an archaeologist, or better still an armchair detective, sifting through dusty layers of fact, fiction, and a whole medley of wild suggestions.

Wulf and Eadwacer – a Saxon text in the Exeter Book, no named author, obscure in background, even more ambiguous in meaning. A word in the very first line may be translated as gift, game, sacrifice or battle, a second liner may mean kill, devour, to mate or to accept as a guest. It is as if directions on a signpost have been swivelled round at random, even altered on purpose so as to cause confusion.

There is one clue however, a linguistic one. This rare text was composed by a woman.

1

I should give the narrator a name – or maybe I won't since she doesn't have one in the poem, nor in the title some later scholar chose: *Wulf and Eadwacer*. For now she must be Anon.

Only nineteen lines of text – less in the original so carefully scribed and tucked into the Exeter Book. Yet these lines provide more puzzles than any bard's song in the mead-hall or Saxon riddler's guessing game. Reams of paper have been used on argument and counter-theory, single words sliced to the root with bitter refutations. If all these were written on skin, how many calves would lie dead?

Yet, in this barren but beautiful scene, anyone may interpret the air.

2

Torrents of rain match her mood. She sits on a hillock of cold, wet grass, buries her face in her hands and sobs. She is wild with love but there is no hope, for her lover is hunted by the law and only her thoughts can follow. Can she save him, clear his name and dodge the brute who would force her to the ground in rape? Bouts of sickness suggest a child.

Wulf, min Wulf, she cries. He will not return. She is at the mercy of every twist.

3

These are waterlogged days. No Dutch engineer has yet drawn up plans, no civil-war prisoners, homesick and shivering, have been sent to the Fens to dredge and reclaim. There are islands here – places whose name endings bring in the smell of salt and eels, marsh and bracken, shallow green pools. Ely, Whittlesea, Welney, Stuntney ... here live men who walk stilt-high in fear of the swamps, pushing small fishing boats into the reeds, hurrying through the darkness of woods where bandits hide.

Wulf is on one island, his girl on another. No wonder she weeps.

4

My thoughts are teased by an image of wool. Was she a peace-weaver, this woman, sent reluctantly in marriage to end a blood-feud, to reconcile enemies who plotted revenge in a Germanic version of *West Side Story*? The text seems too feral and violent for this. Threads in the story rip apart. *One may easily slit that which was never seamed*, says one translator, following the metaphor of cloth.

This could be the landscape of Philomela, who, violated and tongue-less, wove her tale of abuse and agony into a picture that others might read, a web without words but spinning with truth. Is this a tapestry of blood where every stitch is pain?

5

Eadwacer: now here's a name to conjure with – property watcher, heavenly priest, woman's jailer/rapist/lover – or none of these; not a person at all. Text is so easy to tamper with: a comma alters emphasis, a taller initial turns a common to a proper noun.

You have done well, Eadwacer. Mentioned four lines from the end, and then but once, and yet you've pushed and shoved your way into the title (where the author needed none) and made yourself co-star with Wulf, whoever he is.

6

Sacrifice and bloody gifts silt the ditches of these lines. Who called this an elegy, a tale of love and loss? I think the poem reeks of guts, ripped by fangs and teeth.

And overlaying shit and terror are the Saxon Beasts of Battle – Eagle, Wolf, ferocious Boar – they scour the fields for bone.

7

'No!' screams a scholar in my ear. 'You hunt for narrative as if your life depends on a linear shape. This is a riddle, trust me, longer than the ninety or so others in the Book at Exeter, but just as much a puzzle as the ones that suggest the answer is *Storm* or *Sword* or *Ice Inside a Water Butt*. Who knows, it's doubtful, but it might be a puzzle to trick a scurrilous mind that thinks the answer must be *Penis* till a shout of sudden laughter cries '*It's Onion, fool!*'

8

That went past, this may too.

Do *Wulf*'s lines belong elsewhere – an extract from the poem *Deor*? Is *Wulf* a missing section of that lament about a sad minstrel who lost his role and high position and so became a wanderer, one who must endure his grief until the very end?

That went past, he says in refrain.

It is different for us, says the lover of Wulf.

9

Fen-surrounded islands – floating worlds of isolation. Here in marsh and forest were spaces where refugees could hide – if they could endure the pain of arthritis from the constant damp, survive marsh fever and malaria in the heat-wave swamps.

Was Wulf an outlaw in these fens, subject to the common-law's pronouncement: *Caput gerat lupinum* (*May he bear a wolfish head*)? Such a victim could be run through with a sword, bound by vigilantes, held down in a river until he drowned. Many think the name of Wulf provides a clue as to his fate, see him crouched in Ely reeds like Hereward on the run. But surely he'd have offered money, paid a weregild to the injured, cleared his reputation of offence? Wealth could delete the most abhorrent crime.

10

A perfect setting for the sinner, flatlands with cover under a vast grey sky. Equally ideal for the missionary-saints whose obsessive visions reduced them to skin and bone. We hear of Guthlac who, fistful by fistful, dug into the earth of a plundered barrow to make himself an oratory and cell. Here he lived, more than half-starved on his daily scrap of barley bread and cup of muddy water, fierce in his mission but terrified by howling winds and sounds of demons in the night – probably the voices of bitterns and kites, but to him they were fiends from hell.

The Fens are still full of ghosts, even though they have been urbanised and their waters taken from them. I remember a night at Welney – November frost and thick, thick fog. From the sanctuary across the fields the cries of wild geese filled the air, heart-broken spirits, it seemed to me, like those battlefield captives doomed to toil in the Fens in their garments of wet white wool.

It is said that Guthlac, on his deathbed, conversed with angels as scents of ambrosia filled his cell. A morsel of compensation, as St Etheldreda found. Convinced that the tumour on her neck was a punishment imposed on her for wearing a necklace in her youth, she was promised, so documents say, that her body would shine and be incorruptible forever after her death.

11

***What is it ... that you have let pass** such a long time, that you have delayed to come? Why do you not want to remember that I am alone on this earth?*

So begins a letter written in the eighth century by a woman called Bertgyth.

It continues:

How can you afflict the mind of me, who am naught, with constant grief, weeping and sorrow, day and night, through the absence of your love?

Such a letter might be written by any woman to a tardy lover or a dilatory husband. Such a letter might be written by the woman in the poem to Wulf.

In fact Bertgyth, a nun, is writing from Thuringia in Germany to her brother in England. *No other brother will visit me*, she says, *or any other kinsman will come to me ... oh brother, oh my brother, how can you afflict the mind of me.*

There are several letters, in similar tone, written by women to their brothers. Bonds of kinship were important to the Anglo-Saxons and especially so in times of long separation. Themes of loneliness are strong in the writings of nuns and female scholars who were frequently sent, often against their will, into convents or to communities abroad.

There is both sorrow and anger in the letters that survive – as there is in *Wulf and Eadwacer*. Could Wulf be the woman's brother? There are many who go with this interpretation and think the "islands" are monasteries and that the poet-scribe used the act of writing to spill the word-hoard, express a deep emotion.

12

'Not true,' mutters a voice. 'Far-fetched, crazy talk. *Wulf and Eadwacer* is a charm – a charm against tumours or wens as they were called. Look at the language of invocation, the refrains, the narrative ...'

'Rubbish,' cries another. 'It's a metaphor for the Christian Church in its fight against the pagan world. Two islands represent the clash, the differences ...'

'You pluck fantasies from air,' insists a voice of logic. 'The poem is obviously incomplete, parts are missing that would make sense. Look at the damage to the Exeter Book – pages torn out, knife marks all over it, a big circular stain which could be from beer or glue ...'

'No, it is complete.' This from the voice of certainty. 'We are not the audience the poem was intended for. There must be a famous tale behind all this – an old Norse legend perhaps – and an Anglo-Saxon listener would know it well.'

'I have a better theory,' cries a graduate, keen to make his mark. 'None of the things you say are true. There are children in this poem! Wulf is the woman's elder son, he is in danger and so is her infant, the whelp ...'

13

Ah. The whelp. The biggest puzzle of all. *Our wretched whelp*, says the text in translation, *will be carried by a wolf into the woods*. Whose cub? One from a pack of Fenland wolves? A love-child, offspring of Wulf? Of

Eadwacer? A baby conceived in love or lust, marriage or rape? Theories mutter of unwanted children exposed to the elements, left to perish.

On this, the door-leaves of the mouth are sealed.

14

***Where are they now?* An insistent Anglo-Saxon motif**. There are earth-steppers in this poem but their footfalls are light, point in several directions at once, lead only to bones in a peat bog that will never surface, never re-assemble.

And the author of this poem, who was she? Nun? Scribe? Story Teller? Or a woman who once told her tale to someone who liked it, sang it in a mead-hall or two so that others heard, added to it, altered some words, touched the poem with feather-light, finger-tip impressions of yearning and lament?

I saw a man standing, claims a riddle, *a dead man walking who never lived.*

How could this be?

As an image in water, comes the reply – and I wonder if this is a tiny clue to the mystery of *Wulf*: a reflection of light that flickers on a pool for an instant, even as it ripples into shadow and goes.

PART II

Hilde sucked a spurt of blood off her thumb where a holly leaf had stabbed it. Her fingertips, she noticed, were white and numb with cold. 'Leave it to us, Mother Abbess,' said Nerienda, the youngest novice. 'You're scattering berries all over the floor.'

She stepped back to look at the display. The four nuns seemed immune to prickles as they arranged bunches of long-stemmed holly leaves around the altar, bright berries adding warm colour to the frosty day. She decided to leave them to it. Flower arranging was not on her list of roles anyway. She had enough to do with sorting out services and times of prayer, making sure the Rule was observed by the nuns and monks in her charge, checking the two enclaves kept reasonably separate lives. It was already sunset on this particular day and there was still a lot to do.

Left to their own devices, the nuns looped lengths of ivy round the wall, made a garland of holly to hang on the door and slipped in a sprig of mistletoe whose creamy-white, smooth berries showed up against the green and the red. If they whispered of contests when young men would sing in praise of the holly and adolescent girls would raise their voices in celebration of the ivy and their own growing womanhood, there was no one nearby to hear them.

~

'Leave the bucket ice to thaw, Brother Godric,' said Hilde. 'I think the sun is trying to break through.'

'Not to my eyes it isn't,' said Godric, shivering. 'Feels more like snow to me.'

'In good time for Yule, then.' Hilde peered up at the white sky. 'You could be right. I can smell the snow on its way. When I was at the sister house in Chelles I was famous for forecasting the weather – rain, snow, fog – I was always right.'

'That,' said the monk, giving up on the ice, 'is the sin of boastfulness, Mother Abbess. You must forego a spoonful of broth as a penance.' He shivered again in his thin robe. 'I wish I had travelled like you and seen things.'

'Never too late,' said Hilde. 'If you take the advice I am always offering, you will learn all you can about being a scribe. Make your name well known and sought after. You will be so much in demand you will find yourself turning work away and then you may travel wherever you choose. No need to look disbelieving, Godric. Boastful or not, you know I am right. Anyway, off with you now – clean up some wax and scribble away to your heart's content. Riddles, tales, recipes, songs – just write. I can tell you plenty more if you start to run out. At Chelles I was known as the best story teller in the convent ...'

~

There is a problem here for me as author. I want to tell Hilde some background facts, some tidbits to make her story real and relevant to those of us today who have travelled a few more metres down chronology's line.

And yet, how can I interfere? She belongs to Anno Domini 868, that small space of English time when an Abbot or Abbess might have charge over both nuns and monks in the setting of a double monastery – though rarely were the twain supposed to meet.

Hilde appears to have journeyed in Europe, braving bandits and pirates in her spiritual quest, but most people were unlikely to see far beyond their own homesteads; towns were a concept not widely developed and government by a single ruler still waiting for the years to come.

And the mood of the time? The ethos? Artefacts dug up from mead hall and burial ship offer too much of a one sided view. We must not allow Beowulf to be the only one with a say in the re-construction of this Saxon world. If there was turmoil it was quiet at the heart; if there was sorrow there was also a great deal of song.

~

Godric was thinking of Hilde's words as he trudged towards the hut that called itself a scriptorium. He knew she was ambitious, both for him and for the Abbey. He should travel on the Continent, she declared, meet up with learned men, perfect his craft of scribing and bring his knowledge home. The hut, along with several other buildings including the bakehouse and pilgrims' hostelry, should have wood and thatch replaced with stone from the quarry at Barnack. He knew Hilde was good at long-term plans, but was this the time to begin? Always, like a raven's long shadow, the terror of the Norsemen hung over them. It was less than three years since King Edmund had reached an uneasy agreement with those who would plunder East Anglia's realm. Peace in exchange for horses and food. Now, Godric heard, the vast army of marauders was settled in York, busy making the city its own. How long until the raiders got hot and greedy for more? He shuddered. A three day march and hell itself would ascend.

Well, for now, he'd focus on the quiet of the everyday, scour some old parchments with milk and oat bran, scribe a psalm or two for practice, wipe them clean again. The Abbess, as she boasted, had a store of tales to tell to brighten up a cheerless day – stories she remembered from her childhood, songs she'd heard on her travels, twisted riddles to tease the brain. One day, he thought, he would scribe some of these as a surprise for her. Too late for this year, since the following day was Christmas Eve, but maybe as a gift in celebration of Easter or the next Yuletide. Pray God, he thought, that peace in the realm would last.

It was late in the afternoon and he needed the latrine. Demons would be hiding in the pit as full darkness fell, ready to bite the buttocks of the unsuspecting and terrify the nervous with fiendish screams and gulps. Godric hurried to do his business and rush away from the hole.

~

Hilde may have had schemes for Godric but it appears they were among many. Updating the monastery was high on her list of things to do, the outbuildings at least. The Abbey Church itself must have been magnificent then, solid in stone, its massive columns sculpted with angels, foliage and wild capering beasts. A spacious building with light pouring in through the window glass, touching the white marble shrine of Etheldreda, the Abbey's precious saint. Predecessors had spared no expense and neither did Hilde. This church, with its tall tower and huge bronze bell calling the faithful to prayer, needed to be magnificent even if the rest of the site was shabby in wood and straw.

Hilde's predecessors. Magnificence of another kind. A quartet of saints, offspring of Anna, pious king of the Fens. After Werburga the roll call of names is silent for a century or more but no matter. Transcending sisters, cousins and nieces the greatest fame belongs to the above mentioned Etheldreda – twice married virgin, founder of the Abbey, a supposedly incorruptible corpse whose bones brought in both pilgrims and revenue to the whole monastic estate.

Incidentally, I shall be referring to Etheldreda by that name which is a modern version of Æthelthryth – the way she is referred to in most accounts of the time. I considered trying to be respectful to the saint's memory and keep the original spelling but there is something awkward about the look of it. So Etheldreda it will have to be. Not Audrey, an even more up to date version of the name, though I can't imagine how that variation came about.

I need to say more about her, this complex woman. The question of sainthood puzzles me. No doubt she lived an excellent life of prayer and holy deeds but that is not why she was honoured. The reason, I think, concerns the body, viewed in those and later days as a contemptible thing, especially if it was a woman's.

Virginity was crucial to Etheldreda. It underpinned her life and whole identity. The roots of this must have begun with Mary, mother of Jesus, wife of Joseph. Untouched by man before the birth, faith insisted on her purity thereafter with the carpenter doomed to be a husband only in name. Later centuries will go to contradictory extremes by offering Mary a bloodline and a bunch of her sons as step-brothers to Jesus who, in his turn, will be adored as a potential lover for pining women.

It can't have been an easy option for Etheldreda, this virginity. I'm not talking about her own emotions or sexuality. We can only guess at those. She was, however, a princess, a tool in the game of political power, expected to yield and to breed a clutch of sons.

Her first husband, Tolberet, seems to have accepted his role as token. If, before he died after two years of marriage, there were complaints, arguments, attempts at seduction, then they went with him to the grave.

Ecgfrith was another matter. His roars of fury and frustration lasted twelve years and still echo in the annals. We know how Etheldreda would stay awake for hours, praying half the night until her spouse, exhausted, fell asleep. Records describe him as crazy with love for his wife but love, I think, so unreciprocated, must have been painful. Eventually Ecgfrith gave in, allowed his beloved to renounce their marriage, take her vows and become a nun. A false surrender, apparently, since we next hear of him, a few months later, pursuing his ex-wife into the fens, revenge and rape on his mind.

In the swamps and fogs of Ely, Etheldreda at last felt safe; founded the Abbey; became a saint.

~

It was almost time for the evening service but Godric paused, attracted by warm, sweet smells from the bakehouse. Peeping inside he spotted Nerienda and two other young nuns mixing and stirring an assortment of tasty looking ingredients. 'What are you doing, Sisters?' he said, 'you'll be late for Vespers.'

'Just the person I want!' Nerienda wiped her hands on a cloth. 'Go and borrow a key and bring us some dried mint from the storehouse, will you?'

'What for?' The monk stepped over to the long board, his mouth watering at the sight of cranberries, apples and hazelnuts set out in small bowls.

'For tomorrow's honey cakes of course.'

'Honey cakes! But Yuletide Eve's a fasting day!'

'Not after Vespers it isn't. Mother Abbess says we're allowed to have a small celebration. It'll be Mother's Night as well. Don't look so disapproving, Brother Godric. It's an ancient custom and there's no harm in it. Surely it's no sin to nibble a honey cake or two to bring us a goodly new year.'

'They'll taste even better with mint,' said another girl. 'Hurry up and get a move on, Brother. These cakes won't wait.'

~

In Yuletide darkness, two days later, Hilde led the congregation in the service she loved most. Candles glowed and flickered in every alcove and cranny as the voices of forty or more nuns, monks, farmers, foresters, carpenters, women and children swelled in praise. '*Deo Patri sit gloria*,' they sang, and '*O Lux Beata Trinitas*.'

Afterwards, stepping carefully along the narrow path that led to the nuns' quarters, she thought about the Magi who had brought gifts to the child in his coverings of rags, sharing in the mystery and magic of a night such as this when the whole sky shone with so many stars it was impossible to identify the brightest one. 'Smile, Sister,' she said to the young novice who was walking with her. 'Why so sad?'

'I can't help it, Mother,' said Nerienda. 'I've had such dreams the last few nights. I'm terrified that something bad will happen, a sickness with no cure or wild men attacking us in the night and burning us all in our beds.'

'Well,' said the Abbess smiling at her. 'I hope we will hear these wild men coming and not be caught asleep in our gowns. We are in God's hands, child. He is our anchor, our strength. With his help we shall be brave. Now be of good cheer and rest quietly until dawn.'

~

I'll pause for a moment while my characters enjoy this Christmas before they face the further uncertainties of winter, and try and give them some topography, a sense of their place. I've been studying historical maps, trying to overlay a network of rivers and islands on the surface of present day territory which bears little or no resemblance to the Anglo-Saxon Fens. These maps, though fascinating, were not drawn at the time, often not until hundreds of years later. The imagination of a sixteenth century map-maker may well equal mine in scope but also in inaccuracy.

This is what I see, how I think Ely and the Abbey foundation would have looked in 868.

Long before they were drained, the fens were a fresh-water marshland dotted with islands which were areas of higher land free from flooding. Human settlements, reached by boat, were confined to these uplands and marsh edges. Elsewhere, lower, were the tidal washes, mud flats, peat moors, creeks, meres, salt marshes and silt. Perilous places these, thick with reeds and willow where the only way for a man to move sometimes was by walking on stilts.

The double monastery on the Isle of Ely was comparatively safe (from the elements at least) and beginning to look less piecemeal and more structured in the Benedictine design. The Abbey Church was the heart of the land which, with its rich soil, is recorded as covering seven miles by four, providing a haven for the community of nuns and monks as well as for several outlying farms and small dwellings.

~

March was not known as the Ragged Month for nothing and there were days when Hilde, walking from building to building or across the fields, was buffeted by fierce winds that threatened to knock her off her feet. Nevertheless, warmer times were clearly on their way – daffodils were an abundance of yellow against grey stone in the graveyard and snowdrops outlined the long pathway up to the Abbey door.

All seemed good, she thought; the year was following its steady course. The vines had been pruned, the soil smelled good with all the digging, raking and sowing that was going on. The monks who worked as blacksmiths in the foundry complained they could scarcely keep up with the demand for Calf with Trumpet medallions for the hostelry was full most nights with pilgrims who had journeyed many miles to visit the Shrine. For once they brought no bad news with them; even Nerienda was forced to admit that maybe her nightmares, which had seemed so prophetic in winter, were fading in the watery light of spring.

'Listen to that bell,' said Hilde to Godric who was hurrying to catch up with the other monks on their way to Matins. 'To my ears it sounds dull. It would be good to have two of them. A joyful peal, not this monotonous clunk.'

~

After the service the monks and nuns stayed assembled. 'I shall send to Peterborough for help,' said Hilde to the assembled monks and nuns, 'ask if their bell caster may be spared for a month or so to assist us here. They will demand a heavy price but the Abbey can afford it. There is much that needs doing here and it is foolish and displeasing to God that we should hoard our wealth.'

Everyone nodded and gave the hand sign for assent. Nobody argued with Hilde who had the special gift of insight into the wishes of the deity. If any man thought that the making of a new bell might not be top of the list for the heavenly Lord, nor an essential priority for the spending of the Abbey's funds, then he kept his doubts to himself.

'First we must construct the bell pit.' Hilde's eyes were bright with pleasure. 'I shall draw up plans for the digging. Tenants on the farms will help. Sisters, your duties will involve the gathering of beeswax and arranging for the cutting of good strong reeds. I shall send to Lynn for copper and search out the best place for the moulding clay. With God's help and our own firm hands we shall have a peal of two bells before the year's end.'

~

There is a ship at the edge of this story, a long narrow ship filled with men we now know as Vikings. It is a fine vessel but one that will bring no joy to the inhabitants of our small island.

Maybe several longships are rowing out of the fjord. The sky has been overcast for days with a thick mist and I cannot tell at this distance of time and place how many there are. All I know is the leader ship is captained by a man who has been on this voyage before. For convenience I'll call him Asmund though he will go down in history as nameless.

Asmund's presence on the ship is crucial for he will read the patterns of stars, assess which way the wind is blowing, tell by the changing colours of waves when land is near, know which birds always fly close to the shore. Maybe he will recognise landmarks – a rock that resembles a crouching giant, three low hills set close together.

Why is Asmund on this journey? If he has endured it before and returned home safely why is he now setting out again? Has he been promised a good reward if his vessel comes back laden with wheat and tin? Is he aiming for prestige? – the captaincy of a ship such as this would certainly be prestigious. Maybe he is a younger son denied inheritance. Maybe, although this seems unlikely, he is unpopular in his neighbourhood and chooses to escape from some tedious dispute.

Whatever the situation, he is navigating his ship with pride, prepared for all weathers with animal skins for coverings, woollen tents for sleeping on shore, provisions of salted fish and meat, tubs of beer and water – plenty of water.

Who has he left behind? Who will miss him? A wife, a son, girl friend, dog? Many of the crew have gloomy faces as they think of those who are abandoned. Asmund's face shows nothing but determination to see himself and his men through to their destiny, whether that be triumph or a grave in an alien land.

The sky above the ship is clear, blue and cloudless, the fjord's water shines like glass. The oars of the men set a rhythm, strong and well paced. They are on their way.

~

Early May was hot. Unnaturally hot, thought Hilde, with a situation made even worse by the turmoil caused by the bell-casting pit. It was cooler in the gardens where she walked early one morning with Nerienda and three other nuns, but although an array of birds singing from the nearby woods was pleasing and refreshing to her nerves, she was troubled by a low, persistent hum from the cluster of skeps. 'It's the honey flow,' said Nerienda, always knowledgeable on matters of farming, 'They're going frantic, getting ready to swarm.'

'Is someone overseeing them?' Hilde frowned. 'If bees go swarming off into the woods we will lose them! They need to be followed and re-hived quickly. Why are the skeps so near the trees like this? Where is my Bee Guardian? Who *is* my Bee Guardian? Some of these skeps look neglected – straw unravelling all over the place and no shelter for the bees against the heat.'

'I'll find out, Mother,' said Nerienda. 'All the bee-keepers must be out helping the farmers. It's a busy time for them, milking the cattle three times a day on top of everything else. I'm sure the bees won't be forgotten, nor their honey lost.'

'I am more concerned about their wax, Sister,' said Hilde. 'We must have a plentiful supply of candles for the Abbey and beeswax must be of the best.'

~

The rest of the day brought further distress. A very old monk, the oldest in the monastery, had been in the infirmary for seven days, slowly fading away. Hilde had visited him the day before but, for all they had been friends for decades, he did not know her voice. Now news was brought to her in her chamber that he had died, moments after the priest had administered the last rites.

Hilde stood in silent prayer. 'It is we who must suffer the loss,' she said eventually. 'He is in God's care now. The earth was made fairer by his presence as it shall be again when he lies buried in it. Let masses be offered for three days for his dear soul's sake. He shall lie in his shroud during that time by the church porch, on a cross-shaped scatter of ashes. Let holy water be sprinkled each Compline on the earth around him and let his fellow monks recite the psalmist's words *Miserere mei Deus, secundum magnum misericordiam tuam*.'

Holding a candle she walked outside, remembering years of companionship. A bright crescent moon reminded her of a unicorn climbing the cliffs of the sky. Was the soul of her friend climbing high on its way to heaven? She prayed so.

'Mother! Mother!' There was shouting and many people rushing towards her. 'Come at once. We've captured a thief! He's badly injured and will soon be dead!'

~

Bees are the smallest of birds insists a medieval bestiary. A lyrical concept which would have appealed to Pliny, that self-appointed expert on all things. Bees, he declared, were created solely for the sake of man; honey itself fell from the air, accumulating dust and poisonous vapours in its descent to the flowers; sometime later this honey would be gathered in by bees and purified in the hive. How indefatigable they must have been, those bee-scouts of ancient times who would seek distant pastures if nearby flowers drooped. If they happened to journey too far and failed to return before dark, why then, says the scholar, they would make themselves small camps and lie on their backs all night to protect their wings from dew.

A smell of corruption in ensuing centuries taints this idyllic scene. Augustine, that obsessive zealot, encouraged the idea that bees were born out of the rotting and stinking flesh of calves (some say oxen) which, if smitten with brushes, caused worms to form in the flesh. These worms, by some heavenly miracle, would then transform into bees.

Give me Pliny's fantasies any day. His bees would respond to the sound of bronze, gonged and clanging through the air, summoning them to assemble in a vibrant, buzzing crowd. Dead bees, he added happily, could always be revived if covered with mud. They would have done well in the Fens.

~

A massive crowd followed the litter that carried the injured man to the feet of the Abbess. An alarming mob yelling threats and curses, though several women were in tears.

'Stop!' cried Hilde. 'All of you. Stop! Is there one person here who has a clear mind and tongue and can tell me what this man has done, how he is injured?'

Mutterings. One man stepped forward. 'Mother Abbess,' he said, 'this man would steal the bees from your land. He leaned a ladder against a tree in the woods to remove a swarm to a hive of his own but fell to the ground with the swarm clutched tight against his chest. He is now dying, I think, from a thousand stings.'

Hilde studied the man on the stretcher who was gasping frantically for breath through a throat that seemed to be closing up. 'To the infirmary at once,' she said. 'Use your fingernails if needs be and squeeze out the stings. Then bathe him all over with an infusion of lavender, basil, parsley – whatever sweet herbs you can find. And honey too – gather as much honey as you can find in our stores. That will both soothe and draw the poison out.'

'Mother Abbess,' said one, 'he is a felon who would rob us. The crime of bee-robbing must be punished as though the theft were gold.'

Hilde ignored the comment, watching the crowd clear a pathway for the stretcher. 'Who knows this man? Who speaks for him?'

A woman, her face swollen with tears, was pushed to the front. 'He is my son Odel, good Mother. He means no harm to you or to anyone here.' She covered her face with her hands and sobbed.

'Why does he steal our bees that by law belong to the Church?' Hilde's voice was gentle.

'He would make some hives of his own. Sell honey and wax so a few of us may ...'

'May ...?'

'So a few of us may eat.'

Hilde bent low over the woman and touched her hand. 'Go to your son. All this can wait for another day. Pray with me first. *Have mercy upon him O God, according to thy loving kindness, according to the multitude of thy tendernesses.* Now take her to the infirmary. I shall follow soon.'

~

It was a shaken and penitent Odel who stood in front of Hilde four days later. A young man, dark haired and thin of build, he met the Abbess' eyes bravely, waiting to hear her decision.

'By rights,' said Hilde, 'I should turn you over to the authorities for violating our lands of the Church with the crime of theft. The penalty will be severe.'

Odel took a deep breath. 'I deserve whatever fate brings me,' he said. 'I deeply regret the grief I've given you, Mother Abbess, and all the extra suffering that Fate will bring to my sisters and my poor mother.'

'Fate is not fixed, Odel. I believe that with God's help we have the power to change and to shape our destiny. I gather your father is infirm and unable to work.'

Odel nodded. 'As long as he could perform a swineherd's tasks he did them well. Now his legs can no longer carry him from farm to farm nor to the wild forest where pigs graze at harvest time. This burden falls on me and there are mouths to feed.'

'And bees? Why bees? What made you think you had the skill to set up your own secret skeps, sell costly wax and honey enough to feed this hungry brood?'

'I've been a bee-keeper here, Mother Abbess, for five seasons. I have a great deal of skill and if that ladder hadn't slipped from under my feet I would have proved myself.'

'Proved yourself a thief, you mean. I did not realise you knew my bees. I am worried they have become neglected of late. Whose fault is this?'

'Your chief bee-keeper, like my father, has been ailing many months. Men say he will die soon. Nobody oversees your bees, Mother, or manages the swarms. There's no one to sweep the cobwebs out of the skeps or clean them with dung.'

'Enough,' said Hilde. 'You speak well and like a jay have one mouth but many voices. I must repair the broken skin of my estate. Odel, the care of your soul and your good name is now mine to do with as I will. You shall purge yourself of this sin of theft by taking on the role of my chief and trusted bee-keeper, setting to rights and swiftly all that is mis-managed. No – do not speak – prove your gratitude and honesty by doing this work well. Now I must take sustenance and prayer to my ailing steward and to your father as well. The wolf of famine shall not be allowed to prey on my poor doves.'

~

The day could not have been brighter, very warm even for June but with a light breeze that helped to cool the foreheads of haymakers in the fields. Hilde, shading her eyes against the dazzle of scythes, smiled at the children who stepped carefully behind the men as they gathered up armfuls of hay and turned them to dry in the sun. How hard they all work, she thought, knowing there'd be no break in the summer toil for weeks. It would be the Saint's Feast Day soon and she'd heard they were planning a celebration of their own, a small gathering in the market where a travelling pedlar might bring some ribbons and beads and where, at dusk, there might be a dance and a tune or two played on drum and pipe.

There would be services all day in the Abbey, of course, with a visiting bishop and a special new ceremony called Blessing the Throat in honour of Etheldreda who was known to have suffered with the malady. Some of the nuns, no doubt led by Nerienda, would hope for a chance to creep out at some time and watch the merry making from the shadows. Hilde wasn't yet sure if she would allow this. All of them, monk and nun, young and old, had chosen to live by the rigours of the monastic life and it was her duty to make sure they would abide by their choice without too much deviation. 'Choice, what choice?' she imagined Nerienda would say. 'Our fathers choose our lives.'

She hurried on, not allowing herself to admire the purple and yellow flowers growing wild in the meadows, the gold of the corn marigold among the barley, sheep in their pens hot and heavy with soon-to-be shorn fleeces, the flicker and blue of a dragonfly above the pond. She needed to reach the edge of the forest before anyone noticed she was missing, for indeed she was breaking her own rule by wandering around unattended.

In spite of the bright day Hilde's thoughts were anxious as she reached the woods. Even here was much activity for June was the drying month, not only of hay but also of leaves and berries, bark and moss. Overhanging branches must be cut down and carried away in a cart, trees that had fallen in a storm had to be made into logs. Everything needed to be preserved and stored against the hungry months of winter. Already provisions were growing low. The coming harvest would be welcomed with relief.

She thought about Odel who had so nearly lost his life in these woods, stealing a swarm of bees. How well he was doing now; the Abbey's bees were blessed by the care he took of them. A quiet young man but with an air of authority about him. Many turned to him for advice on all manner of things. One to be trusted, thought Hilde, and she needed him now.

The hostelry, as always, had been full most evenings with pilgrims who, on foot and by boat, made their damp and weary way across the Fens to Ely. The news they brought with them was increasingly grim: sudden, isolated raids on hamlets and villages further to the north, some nuns who had been caught while out walking, raped and thrown in a ditch to die, fires that ravaged the hay in the fields and left it as blackened stubble.

It was time for action. The Lord, no doubt, would watch over them but he might be distracted by other matters and forget to protect the Abbey from raids. Hilde knew she must be practical and plan desperate measures to meet a possible desperate situation. Secret paths through the woods must be created, small flat-bottomed boats built and hidden in the reeds, even a tunnel near the Abbey could be dug or an underground shelter made. Odel was the one to do it, to make plans and put them into practice, just in case. Just in case.

Hilde felt a huge burden lifted from her shoulders. Even the thought of doing something was a comfort. The forest was suddenly full of wing-beats, the air resonating with invisible birds. 'What would I wish for,' she thought, 'except for always this.'

~

Where are they now, those bold longships, those eagles of the north? Asmund has been leading them for two months. I don't know what routes he has taken or what he has seen, but all the time he is getting closer to Ely, one small island in a larger island's realm.

Maybe one of the ships is missing? However brave and strong a team, waves in a thunderstorm can be merciless. In a struggle to the death with water and wind the hardiest eagle will sink. If this has happened it must be shocking for Asmund, the thought of his men struggling, drowning, their bodies ravaged by rock and ice, bone and flesh picked clean by fish or washed ashore upon an alien land, far away from ancestors and gods, to be tossed un-lamented and un-marked into some mass grave.

I have been picturing Asmund and his ships still at sea, days away from sight of land, exhausted but unable to sleep on the pitching deck, weary of eating salted meat, hungry for hot food and dreaming of roasted sheep or slices of red deer.

This may be so but more likely he is manoeuvring his way along the coastline and around the edges of England, using his nose to smell trees, plants, earth. Any shallow river he finds is his to navigate and explore; the shallow draft of his ships will let him find places no other sea-going vessels are able to reach. Needing no harbour, he can land anywhere on the sand and gravel of some shelving beach where his men may disembark, pitch tents, hunt, makes fires, eat. Maybe his orders are to travel overland, build huge wooden rollers for transporting the ships, join the Great Army restless and fidgeting in York – but for now he has time to lurk, lay tracks, mark out waterways and causeways where a willow timber bridge may be rapidly assembled. He is mapping the layout, getting a feel for land. Like a pig that roots for truffles, he will snuffle and find.

~

'Here is a riddle for you,' said the scop. 'Who will be the first to tell me the name?'

My robes are silent when I step onto earth's
green grasses or disturb the still waters.
Sometimes my garments lift me up and into
the clouds of the upper air, high in the sky
over the woodlands and houses of warriors.
Then my garments will sing, a clear, bright
melody and I am a messenger, a spirit
moving over the land. Ask me my name.

Village children giggled and whispered among themselves, pushing each other to the front of the group to speak. 'A swan!' called out a pink-cheeked child who Hilde recognised as Odel's youngest sister. The scop smiled approval at her as all her friends clapped.

'I knew that,' said Nerienda. 'That was too easy.'

'Shush.' Hilde made the hand sign for silence. 'I am not sure it is even right for us be here, Sister, let alone taking part. This evening belongs to the villagers to celebrate our blessed saint in their own way. We are onlookers, only here by their kind invitation.'

'I'm very glad we are here.' Godric smiled at her. 'This is a wonderful chance for me to hear some of the old riddles and tales. Takes me right back to the days when I must have lived near a river.'

Others in the small group standing behind the villagers murmured agreement. 'Well,' said Hilde, 'I must confess I had forgotten that riddle. How it all comes back. The hours I spent as a young woman watching swans on the river glide by. Beautiful creatures.'

'Beautiful but dangerous.' Godric shuddered. 'I've a memory of a swan attacking a child who had gone too near the nest. Everyone screamed and the child was felled to the ground like a sapling in the wind.'

'I hope you are taking proper note, Godric.' The Abbess put on her sternest look. 'I am not letting you wander about and have special leisure time like this if you are not going to practice your skills and write it all down.'

'Wait till you see what I've been doing. My scribblings may be rough but they're crafted with care.'

'Brother, be quiet.' Nerienda made frantic signs. 'The scop's about to sing. Please, Mother, may we stay a while longer?'

'A short time then. We must respect one who has travelled a great distance to honour us with his music and words. Brother Godric, I will speak further with you. I have been musing on a plan.'

~

Hilde's idea of a short time stretched into a much longer interval, the scop holding them entranced with his riddles and later on with some seafaring tales. It was only when he put away his lyre and moved back into the shadows to make space for those waiting to dance with whistle and drum that the small group from the Abbey was persuaded to leave.

Godric moved away like one in a trance, still in the world created by the scop's final poem in which a minstrel lamented his destiny whereby he had lost his privileged position as the favourite of a lord. Brought low and shunned by everyone he encountered, he was doomed to be a wanderer, his poems not listened to, his songs unsung.

That went past, this may too. The refrain echoed in Godric's head, his fingers itching with the urge to scribe the tale onto wax or parchment, to make it his own and add it to his growing collection. At the same time he was uneasy. The minstrel in the poem had been the victim of Fate, his dream broken by the fulfilment of a destiny over which he had no control. The pattern of his suffering was laid down from before his birth. What, he wondered, did Fate have in store for any of them?

He glanced behind him at the villagers who were now merrily dancing under the stars. Odel was the lead musician, playing the tune on his bone whistle, tapping the rhythm with his foot. Nerienda, Godric realised, was also gazing at the scene, trailing several steps behind the others as if the music was drawing her back into the circle of moonlight where the young man stood.

~

I've been thinking about accuracy – historical accuracy in a work of fiction and how important it is to get the context right, to appreciate the social setting of the time. Otherwise one might just as well invent a character with twenty-first century values and attitudes and drop them into the middle ages, for example, dressed up in chain mail or doublet and hose.

So I am wary of novels that call themselves historical but depict characters who would have been totally out of place in the societies in which they are set. Yet an anachronism may be subtle. We would laugh out loud if a narrative had someone use a mobile phone at Agincourt or send a text to Henry VIII reporting infidelity by his latest wife. Yet we frequently accept and don't cringe when attributes more akin to a suffragette are given to a medieval bride who refuses conjugal rights to her drunken, brutal lord. Similarly, a Saxon nun with downcast eyes is often revealed as feisty and wayward, a feminist under the skin.

This is why Nerienda bothers me. Against my wishes she seems to be becoming just that. I allowed her to enter this story as someone young and light hearted, a balance against the serious minded, older folk. Now she is demanding a bigger role for herself, questioning her family's decision to place her in a convent and endow the Abbey with a goodly sum for her keep.

Even more unsettling, I find that in spite of being a novice and making promises (soon to be vows) of chastity, she appears to be developing an infatuation for Odel whom Hilde has placed in a position of trust. She seems to be requiring me to write her into a theme of love, to fill some of this dour Abbey with romance.

How plausible and accurate are this girl's demands? She certainly does not belong to the present century, nor to any part of the world where choice is a human right to which many people cling and in whose name they demonstrate, speak out and fight in order that others may have the same freedoms. Maybe Anglo-Saxon society offered more gender equality than people once thought. There were many strong women, as documents show – abbesses like Hilde for example. What did life in a convent offer them? A structured, intellectual life? The appeal of ritual, of ceremony and routine? A status to be looked up to, that of a Bride of Christ?

But maybe none of this for Nerienda. As needs be then. Feelings in this quiet place are beginning to grow like the circle of moonlight where Odel is standing, where the last notes of the lyre linger, a melancholy tune.

~

A slither of pale light behind the trees was the only hint of dawn. Hilde, waiting by the horse and cart, enjoyed the silence. The making of the Abbey's new bell would soon start up again with its daily arguments and commotion, and nearby fields would be full of chatter and shouts as the back-breaking work of clearing weeds and raggedy plants began. For now, however, she could enjoy the quiet of a night's passing, muse on the service of Lauds just finished in the church, consider her God before the cares of the day.

'Look, we've got Ellette! Dearest Ellette!' Nerienda, hurrying along the path with three other nuns, ran up to the small and sturdy mare, hugging its neck tightly, smoothing the tangled black mane. 'Dear little elf.'

Hilde studied the horse. 'She may be little but I would hardly call her elf-like.'

'Oh but she is! Look at her eyes. You can tell she remembers her life in the forest when she roamed wild and free with goblins.'

'Well we do not want any roaming wild and free now. Our safety depends on her strong back and steady hooves. Here comes our carter. In you climb, sisters. I hope you have all broken your fast with enough griddle cakes. There is a long way to go.'

By noon they had travelled halfway on their journey to St Mary's in Willingham for the enclosure service. The sun was high overhead and all the nuns in the cart were wilting in their hot, dark robes. All, that is, except Nerienda who was still as bright as she had been at dawn, prattling away like a sparrow that chirrups and tweets in the hedge. 'If the first week of August be warm, the winter will be white and long,' she sang in reply to a comment about the day's heat.

Hilde studied the girl. There was something unsettling about her, the way her eyes glittered and in her incessant chat. As Abbess it was her duty to be aware of all that was going on, not only in the outward show of the many people in her care but also in their lives and secret selves. In any case she could hardly have failed to pick up the vibrations between Nerienda and the young man, Odel. The air between them quivered whenever they saw each other or had any kind of contact. Two days previously the girl had wanted to take part in preparations for the Lammas festival but Hilde had been forced to deny permission. A joyful occasion, usually, when the precious early fruits of the harvest were celebrated and the first sheaves of corn, ground up and baked into loaves of bread, were brought as offerings into the church. Nerienda, whose arts as a cook seemed stronger than her skills as a future nun, had begged to be allowed to make a loaf owl with berry eyes. Hilde had refused, instructing her instead to keep a solitary all-night vigil in the church after the service ended. This would be the time when she, as Abbess, would need to turn a blind eye to the ancient village custom of breaking the Lammas bread into quarters, placing the parts at the four corners of the barn to protect the newly garnered grain. Nerienda's head, thought Hilde, was full enough already of fancies and distractions without the influence of charms and magic rituals drifting in.

'Can't go much further now,' said the carter. 'That was the easy part. From here on it's far too marshy and dangerous for Ellette's hooves, let alone the weight of the cart with all of you in it.'

'You have both led us well.' Hilde eased herself out of the cart. 'I would not expect the pair of you to go with us any further. I shall lead us the rest of the way on foot. I know the way across the marshes as well as any guide and have taken many a band of nervous pilgrims through. Will you be here on our return tomorrow?'

'Myself or someone most certainly will.' He helped the trio of elderly nuns to clamber out of the cart. Nerienda, ignoring his hand, jumped lightly down. 'God be with you on your journey, Mother Abbess. Mind you walk slowly, one at a time and make sure no one takes a single step away from the track.'

They had eaten most of their bread and apples on the cart but they paused for a moment now to quench their thirst and dampen their dry lips with water from the leather pouches on their belts. Ahead of them through the huge reeds lay the Aldreth marshes with their ancient trackways and markings of settlements stretching back, so legends said, to the days of iron. Further ahead in the soft-blue distance was the river, glistening in the sunlight, busy with water birds, lined with rows and clumps of the alder from which the place took its name.

~

Let's leave Hilde and her companions to make their weary and perilous way. Fortunately it's August and the marsh, though slippery and likely to sink under their feet, is not too treacherous and they are able to reach the bank of the river and pause for a while under the canopy of alder trees while they consider the precarious river bridge. Maybe Hilde remembers the medicinal properties of the Alder leaf for easing the swelling in tired feet and pulls some down to tuck inside their shoes. Maybe Nerienda alarms them all by reminding them of ghouls and goblins, evil spirits in the alder, bandits that lurk behind a tree ready to cut their throats. Maybe they remember old, old tales about the sap in a cut-down alder, sap the colour of blood.

And maybe one of the elderly nuns whimpers with fright at the prospect of crossing the river bridge which, though built up with alder wood is still partially under water, not exposed to the weakening air. Nerienda does not know, of course, that one day the city of Venice will prove the strength of the wood and rise, magnificently strong on its piles of alder, but she does know that this temporary bridge will hold them, lead them across to the other side, away from her island that she would like to forget about if only for a day – at any rate she holds the hand of the timid nun and takes her across.

And none of them know that not too many years down the line a rebel will discover the secret paths that Odel is now developing in the woods and marshes of Ely and will find his way to safety there while soldiers, determined to capture this rebel and slaughter him like a wild animal, will build and re-build this river bridge, make it a causeway that leads not only out of but into the island that is the subject of our tale. This rebel, like others before him, will be betrayed by one in the know and Ely's secrets revealed.

Maybe all of this. Hindsight is easy. Playing with “what ifs” can be fun – at a distance; for us at any rate. For now the little party of nuns is met by another horse and cart and taken, through the mixed light of early evening, to St Mary’s where the Ceremony of Enclosure for an anchoress will take place the following day. Here they are greeted, welcomed warmly, given some nourishing food and later led to their beds.

Except for Hilde who will join the would-be anchoress as she kneels in the candle-lit church, having made confession and been shriven and who now will keep a vigil of prayer all night. Tomorrow morning this young woman will be enclosed.

~

‘We must be diligent in our thoughts, words and deeds and ever watchful against the snares of the devil,’ droned the bishop as he launched into his sermon before the Service of Enclosure. ‘We must remember the shortness of this life, this difficult path of our journey, the good that we do which is so meagre and our sins which are many. One day we will die, that is written and certain as is the stern Day of Judgement that will face us all and consign us, according to our merit and the grace of Almighty God, to the pains and sorrows of hell or to the blessing of an eternal reward in the bliss of heaven.’

St Mary’s was packed with dignitaries and special guests, the air thick with incense and heat. Nerienda felt her thoughts beginning to drift. She knew that for the soon-to-be anchoress – the focus of everyone’s attention as she knelt in front of the altar – this would be her last chance ever to be part of the outside world. From now on she would only hear sermons, liturgies, canticles and antiphons via the thickness of stone, receive the Sacrament through a window barely a slit.

‘This day our sister has chosen to see the face of God shine more brightly in heaven.’ The bishop launched further into rhetoric. ‘Evil beasts of temptation may ravage and prowl in the streets outside and in the depths of her innermost soul but she, with constant prayer and Divine help, will fight boldly with the lion of pride, the snake of poisonous envy, the unicorn of anger, the bear of sloth, the fox of covetousness, the sow of gluttony and the scorpion with the tail of stinging lechery that is lust.’

He paused, gasping for breath, to wipe the sweat off his face. ‘I exhort you all to pray for her that she may fight the temptations of this wilderness as did Our Lord when he confronted the vile machinations of Satan for forty days and forty nights in the desert.’

She looks too fragile to fight any wild creature, inner or outer, thought Nerienda. The face of the anchoress was hidden by a black veil but she knelt stiffly upright, unmoving, and the lighted candle in her hand was still. With some anxiety Nerienda considered the bishop's request, made before the service began, that she, as the youngest novice present that day, should later follow the procession and carry the candle into the anchoress's cell where, with the closing of the door, the light would be extinguished.

As the deer pants for streams of water,
so my soul pants for you, my God.

The congregation stood, the voices of the choir swelled like birdsong.

Why, my soul, are you downcast?
Why so disturbed within me?

The church was hot and Nerienda could scarcely breathe with the bodies squashed in around her, but at the words of the psalm she shivered. All the excitement of the last two days had gone. Rays of early morning sun came darting in through the open door but the bishop's final words hammered in her brain. This young girl, this anchoress, he had said beforehand, had chosen to live until death in the cold isolation of her cell where she would 'deliberately forgo the sunshine with the rest of nature's gifts.'

I say to God my Rock,
'Why have you forgotten me?
Why must I go about mourning,
oppressed by the enemy?'
My bones suffer mortal agony
as my foes taunt me,
saying to me all day long,
'Where is your God?'

Nerienda clasped her hands tightly together to hide the trembling.

~

'The girl's face was hidden by a black veil,' says the description of this anchoress and I think it will always stay hidden. Even if the veil is lifted and her features revealed I doubt if we should be any the wiser as to her personality, motives, moods or thoughts. The back story to her narrative must remain dark.

I could conjecture. Somewhere in this tale there is money involved. The acceptance of an anchoress into a religious community invariably depended on a large donation from her family's estate, a dowry for a Bride of Christ. The will of her father may have played some part in this girl's decision.

And yet it is unlikely to have been a totally reluctant choice. Before anyone could enter an anchorhold there would be weeks of preparation, a time for probing questions, the strength of religious faith put to the test. There were alternatives as well. A woman could enter a convent, a man could choose the monastic life. The sacrifice of kinship would still be involved and there would be many harsh privations, but at least there would be the company of others and the freedom of open air.

Records show there were many more anchoresses at this time than anchorites. A man who was drawn to this way of life could choose to be a hermit, didn't need to follow the route of enclosure. This choice does not seem to have been available for women. Perhaps they were assumed to need protection, be too weak to face the dangers of the "desert" or the "wilderness" outside. This seems debatable to me. More fearful, I think, to be enclosed by walls of the body and the imagination.

There was considerable status attached to the role of anchoress. Although there are horror stories about cells being bricked up and the inhabitant almost literally being buried alive, most anchorholds had two or even three small windows (albeit covered with dark cloth) and those outside who were in need of spiritual guidance could converse with the anchoress and receive her words of wisdom. Maybe this enhanced importance, this sense of being for once in charge and in control, might appeal to someone who suffered from feelings of inadequacy, had a low self image.

It is all conjecture. I have a theory that the answer lies in a longing for those spaces of otherness that Michael Foucoult calls heterotopias. Spaces that have more layers of meaning than immediately meet the eye, spaces that are simultaneously physical and mental – not good, not bad, but different.

Maybe the anchoress in this narrative is living a daydream, a wishful, visionary reverie that she is reluctant to be woken from. If this daydream involves physical hardship and the annihilation of identity, then she is willing to let it happen.

And yet how can this happen when the enclosed conditions she is choosing for her future existence must act as a force that will shape the very identity she is trying to submerge?

~

'Receive me, O Lord, according to your word.' The anchoress, kneeling on the altar steps, spoke so softly that everyone, except the dignitaries in the front rows, leaned forward to hear. The bishop, tall and splendid in his ceremonial robes, sprinkled holy water on the girl's dark kirtle and veil.

'Receive me, O Lord, according to your word.' She moved towards the altar as she recited these words, placing her bright candle on the white cloth. Nerienda tensed, knowing her role in the ceremony was near.

'Receive me, O Lord, according to your word.' The anchoress lay face down before the altar, her arms outstretched in the shape of a cross. '*Veni Creator Spiritus*,' chanted the choir.

Hilde touched Nerienda gently on the shoulder, nodding at her to take the candle from the altar and follow the procession of bishop, anchoress, prelates and choir down the nave. She herself followed behind with the other nuns and the rest of the congregation, moving slowly and with reverence but anxious not to miss a second of what lay ahead.

Outside the church the procession moved round to the shaded north side where the exterior door of the anchorhold was situated. By now Nerienda was shaking with nerves and the flame of the candle flickered. There was silence at the entrance to the cell except for two rooks loud in a tree. 'Come, my people,' intoned the bishop, reading from Isaiah, 'enter your chambers, and shut your doors behind you; hide yourselves for a little while until the fury has passed by.' He made the sign of the cross over the open door. 'Who is the one that wishes to enter here?'

The girl stepped forward. 'I offer and give myself to the mercy of God in the order of an anchoress to live in his service according to the rule and here, in the presence of you, worthy father in God, I make my obedience.'

Her voice was low but steady. With the bishop sprinkling holy water, a priest swinging a censer, the anchoress, a nun either side of her, moved into the cell. Nerienda followed behind with the candle held high.

It was gloomy inside and stone cold. The first thing anyone saw in a dark corner of the cell was a shallow open grave. Nerienda had been prepared for this, knew that one of the anchoress's duties every day was to deepen her own grave by scraping a small amount of earth from the pit with her hands, but she still gasped in shock and her heart beat fast.

The anchoress knelt. The bishop beginning the Last Rites, anointed the girl with oil on her eyelids, ears, nostrils, lips, hands and feet each time saying 'Through this Holy Oil, and through the great goodness of His mercy, may God pardon you whatever sins you have committed by evil use of sight, hearing, taste or touch.'

At a signal the girl laid herself down in her shallow grave. 'Let all who are present,' continued the bishop, 'repeat these words after me: This shall be her rest for ever.'

'This shall be her rest for ever.' Nerienda's lips were dry. The bishop, offering his hand to the anchoress to raise her to a kneeling position, bent down and gathered a handful of soil from the grave, sprinkling it over her head and garments with the words 'From dust you were made and into dust you shall return.'

He gestured to Nerienda to extinguish the candle as he and the rest of the clergy turned to leave the cell. The anchoress, still kneeling on the hard floor, bowed her head and clasped her hands together in prayer. Nerienda, her eyes blurred with tears, looked back at her one last time. Then she snuffed the candle out.

~

It was late morning when the group from Ely set out on the journey back. Fortunately the day was cooler than it had begun, the early sun giving way to an overcast sky befitting the funereal mood affecting all those who had attended the service. The journey by horse and cart to the river crossing at Aldreth was made almost in silence, everyone dozing or lost in their own thoughts. Nerienda, as before, helped the nuns across the rickety bridge then trudged moodily across the marsh. As they neared the higher ground of Haddenham, Hilde was glad to see Ellette waiting patiently for them beside the cart with Odel as their guide. At least, she thought, the sight of him will cheer the novice up. She glanced at the despondent face of the girl. Nerienda, however, saying nothing, climbed into the cart and sat there, hunched up.

Odel drove them safely back to the Abbey in the growing darkness, proud to take them a different way through the forest and point out some of the secret tracks he and his team of helpers had discovered or made. Looking behind her Hilde could see no hint of the path, nothing but undergrowth and thick canopies of huge dark trees. 'Heaven help anyone who comes here on their own,' she said. 'We would be lost without you, Odel.'

'It's not too difficult to find your way. For weeks I've been watching our friend Reynard, that wily old fox. He knows how to hide himself cunningly in shadows or enlarge an existing burrow to make his den. He may pad along softly but he's always alert to any hint of danger.'

'Well those of us who can, shall follow your example and be like the fox. As for the rest, Odel,' Hilde glanced at the nuns, 'you must watch out for them and be their guide.'

'I shall. I give you my word,' he said.

~

Godric was getting himself a reputation in the community for remembering, in detail and from a single hearing, the words of riddles and tales. This encouraged Hilde in her belief that he would make a fine scribe who would benefit from extra time and opportunities to work on his craft for the good of the Abbey. However, deep down, Godric was troubled. The past, his own past in particular, was a mystery to him. Something said or seen might trigger a flash of memory as when the riddle of the swan on the Saint's Feast Day brought back a sudden glimpse of himself as a small boy gazing at a river scene. Where the river was, why he was there or what had happened next was a blank. It seemed to him he had always lived in this monastery, even been born there, but Hilde assured him this wasn't so although she too was vague about when he had actually arrived.

Thinking about the swan riddle reminded him that it was Odel's youngest sister who had guessed the answer. How well that young man was doing now, a thief turned hero, caring and dependable, respected by monk and farmer alike. It was thanks to Hilde, of course, who had recognized Odel's qualities, had nurtured the goodness in him and brought out the best as she did in everyone. Godric didn't know how he would survive a day without her.

He thought about the charm against bees which he had heard people muttering, and still remembered word for word from the occasion when Odel was lying on his sick bed, half dead from the stings.

Settle down on the earth
you victorious women,
never go flying wildly

into the woods.
May you be as mindful
of my welfare
as every man is
of sustenance and home.

At the time he had wondered why a swarm of bees should be compared to women. None of the females he knew showed any signs of "stinging". All those in the double monastery seemed gentle and calm to him, not in the least bit vicious or wild. Now he wondered if the bee-women in the rhyme were victorious because of their strength. Hilde, he thought, most certainly was strong, with an inner strength that kept her busy and organized with incessant practical and spiritual tasks while, at the same time, she cared for everyone else's needs.

'Day dreaming again are you, Brother?' Hilde's voice behind him made Godric start.

'I must confess I was, Mother Abbess. I was on my way to the bell pit to see how everyone's doing and I started thinking about swans and bees.'

'Of course you did,' said Hilde. 'Let us go there together. I have some ideas I want to discuss with you anyway. A plan I have been considering for some time.'

~

For six months the new bell for the Abbey had occupied every moment of time that could be spared from farming or prayer. The bell-caster from Peterborough had paid two visits to Ely, the first to offer general advice, the second, still ongoing, to be there on hand with advice at critical moments. Godric had taken little part in the bell's making, Hilde preferring him to use his hands for delicate work with stylus and quill, but he realised it had been constantly in the background to his thoughts as had the smell and dust of clay. Wood fires had been burning non-stop to heat up tools for smoothing and shaping wax over the core of the bell, preparing it for its later double coats of clay.

Now the core of the bell was in its pit, carefully lifted up from the platform and lowered on strong ropes by twenty of the village's strongest men. Here it would stay while the furnace in the small nearby foundry was stoked up to the fiercest heat possible that would melt metal.

The top of the pit was boarded over with strong logs, Hilde being terrified of accidents. Inside, on what would be the rim of the bell, Godric thought of the words of dedication set in raised letters on wax: *To the blessed saints Felix and Etheldreda. Ely. The Year of Our Lord Eight Hundred and Sixty Nine.*

~

And so the Ely bell lies in its pit, ready to be cast, cooled, roped and heaved up to the surface, fitted with a clapper, tuned, prepared for christening in a great ceremony and then raised even higher up to the top of the Abbey tower to join its fellow bell and ring out across fields and rivers, marshes and woods. This is the plan arranged for it. Fate, for the moment, is in the hands of men.

So much for the bell. All seems clear. For Asmund however, who I imagine far away in York having joined the Great Army, the future seems as foggy as this late September day. In previous months he had been his own master, in charge of several ships as they manoeuvred their slow and careful way along the rocky coastline. Now the crews are disbanded, their oaths of fellowship sworn to each other on a ring of iron are loosened, the huge ships hidden and the men dispersed, absorbed into the magnificent Army beast.

Now he waits for further orders, exercises daily to toughen his muscles, practices some archery skills, drinks and dices with a few companions late at night or sits around the fire and listens to music played on a lyre or goat's horn. Who knows, he might even compose a tune himself.

But in the background all the time, like the rhythm of his heartbeat, is the longing for honour, the need to suffer whatever fate brings but to suffer it well. How fearful it would be, he thinks, to die as he must but to die in shame as a laggard or deserter, to have his name inscribed in stone on a monument as one disgraced. He clenches his fists at the thought. His name must be forever mentioned with pride by his kin, the mantle of honour must fall on the shoulders of his son, if he should ever have one.

And possibly, on this foggy day, he comforts himself by remembering tales about his ancestors who had faced their deaths with courage even if they sank fathoms deep in a drowning sea, even if the gods did not look favourably upon the battle which slew them. The threads of their honour, he knows, are woven tightly with his.

A melody thought to be from this century and notated on wood, has been passed down to us. "*I Dreamt Me a Dream*" is the title it has been given. I like to think of Asmund playing this, dreaming his own dreams, waiting bravely for the threads of his destiny to twist and tangle with those of others, even if they lead to his own inevitable death.

~

The Great Army and later generations of Vikings have left a permanent mark on Jorvik, the present day city of York. When, as a tourist, I experienced the sights, sounds and smells of the Viking Jorvik Museum, one of the most poignant things for me was a skull in a display case with a re-constructed model of the human being it once was, placed next to it.

There is a poem at the heart of *The Wulf Enigma* as well as riddles, songs and tales, so hopefully it won't be out of place if a few of my own verses creep in from time to time. An over-active imagination? Perhaps, but that night, after the Viking Experience, I looked at the postcard I'd bought of the young farmer as he might have been and thought about the skull in its sad glass case. It felt as if he was speaking directly to me:

Jorvik Man

Let me go back to the rubble.
Shovel it all upon me again.
I no longer can hear the iron of hooves.
There is much comfort in mud and in rock,
fragment of pale bone.

Give me the feel of berry and seed,
dry stag horn, wet vegetation,
sharp bright buckle, broken clay,
small beads of amber and jet.

Give me the smell of leather and dung,
herring and salt tang of sea.

Let me go back to the rubble.
I am Jorvik man.
Leave me.

~

'I have spent many moons planning this, Brother Godric,' said Hilde. 'The last thing I want is for you to offer me foolish objections.'

'Forgive me, Mother Abbess. I did not intend to annoy you. I just can't take it all in.'

'Well, I will say it once more, slowly, and you may ask me three questions and then no more. I want you, with two brothers of your own choice, to journey to Lindisfarne and live for a time with our Brothers in Christ. While you are there you must observe and learn all you can about the scribe's craft. Fill your head to the brim with knowledge and bring it back to us here. I have many dreams for this Abbey. Next year we shall build and grow and one day become a centre for learning that will be the envy of all men. You shall be our pathfinder, our guiding light.'

'Mother Abbess, you honour me too much. My mind is heavy with doubt but my heart is full of such joy that I have no words to express it.'

'Then you had better find your words again and rapidly. Before you go, and when you return, I shall expect you to write and write until the bones in your fingers cramp and freeze. Many nights lately, Godric, I have dreams about a book, a radiant and jewelled book, written here in this Abbey to the glory of God.'

'Mother, shall we have the time for such a wonderful task? Who knows how many winters, or how few, lie ahead for us?'

'Then ours must be the cradle and fulfilment shall be the Lord's. That was the first of your questions by the way. What else?'

'I have no more. My trust is in you and in Almighty God. May He be the light on my path.'

'Amen to that. Now come with me. There is a very small cell down here below the crypt – be careful of those steps – hardly anyone knows it is here. At the moment, as you will see, it is full of stones and bundles of straw. I shall have it cleared and then I want you to store all your scribing tablets and parchments here. You must practice your skills, Godric, practice and learn. I know you have already gathered many riddles and songs and I shall tell you many tales, some true, some fanciful. Use them for practice and one day you shall scribe the Gospels of Our Lord. Mind your footing on all those stones. This cell will be perfect for storage and you can use it as a workroom as well. Bring your inks in here and I will see if I can obtain some more parchment scraps. It will all work out well.'

~

It is difficult to know, after more than eleven hundred years, how many of the texts that have passed down to us and survive today are Godric's. Documents will have been copied and re-scribed many times in the intervening years, spelling errors made, passages left out by mistake and deliberate changes inserted, for in those days nobody worried too much about accuracy or copyright. Generations of scribes, freely and creatively, altered all manner of texts as they thought fit.

Out of those many anecdotes told on various occasions by Hilde and scribed by Godric, only fragments remain and even then the authentication is in doubt. What I shall do is try and piece them together, contradictory and confusing as they are, keeping the mood of the tales as I think they would have been intended, but putting them down myself, as if I were the author, in a more up to date language and style.

Like a medieval scribe I shall also allow myself to be creative, give myself plenty of scope.

~

Hilde's Fragment 1

They call this place the Isle of Eels and on very hot days or when the wind blows in a certain direction, the air is full of the smell – salty, gritty and thick with mud. The island is dependent on eels, always has been for as long as men remember. Poorest tenants on the Abbey lands pay their rent to the Church in eels, boys on the estate from the age of five are given quick-fire lessons in skinning, girls carry buckets of white flesh to their mothers to fillet and stew. No islander dares tire of the fishy-sweet taste for it is his livelihood.

Once this island was even thicker with forest where the sun rarely had chance to penetrate the growth. A harsh, damp place where sickness bred in the marshes and where an unwary footfall could sink a man to his neck and above. A grim place, fitter for wolves than men.

To this island came a girl. Her name is not given to us but legends say she may have been a princess from a fighting kingdom. No place for a girl unused to the Fens, especially one as lonely and wretched as she must have been – far from her kin, guarded by strangers, a pawn in the game of warfare, a token offered in a spurious hope of peace.

~

Instructed by Hilde to chase up the Abbey's monthly consignment of eels, Godric accompanied Nerienda and two other nuns to the busy quayside by the river at Stuntney. The young novice, glad to enjoy even a small measure of freedom from routine, seemed in a brighter mood than she had been in recent weeks since the ceremony of enclosure.

'You are so lucky, Brother Godric,' she said. 'I wish I could travel like you.'

'I know I'm fortunate.' Godric manoeuvred a way for them across the quayside, making sure the women didn't slip on fish slime or trip over coils of rope. 'I'll have a lot to do, many things to find out about. It will be hard work but I'm prepared for that.'

'I think you are very brave to go.' Nerienda stopped, fascinated, as always, by the paraphernalia of nets, poles, timber and wicker work that made up the series of eel traps on the river.

'Maybe it is my destiny.' Godric smiled at her. 'My destiny or God's will, anyway. He knows what he has chosen for me just as he has chosen that you should take your holy vows.'

He glanced at the girl, unsure what effect his words would have. Nerienda, shrugging, turned away.

'Sister,' he continued, 'Mother Abbess has said that as we are so near your family home she is willing to give us permission to pay a short visit to your father. Would that please you? I am sure he will be glad to know how dutifully you are following his wishes. It will be a proud moment for him when he comes to see you take your vows.'

Nerienda shook her head. 'He won't care. My brothers are the only ones who give him pride. I was sent here as a novice so there'd be no further need to provide for me. Thank you for the thought, Brother Godric, but I have no wish to go visiting today.'

'Stay here then, with the Sisters, and I'll go and barter for our barrels.' Godric, stepping carefully across a mess of blood and overflowing guts, disappeared into a hut to talk to the man responsible for the monastery's supplies of smoked and pickled eels.

Nerienda, ignoring instructions, walked over to the muddy banks by the water's edge. Three children crouched here, digging around in the mud with their barbed and pronged spears hoping to locate an eel nest. One of the boys gave a shout, lifting up his spear with a frantic, wriggling eel on it.

'Poor thing. What a waste.' Nerienda turned away in disgust.

~

Hilde's Fragment II

The girl sent as peace-weaver sat on a log watching a slow line of ducks on the river being carried downstream by the drift. Occasionally one would up-turn, scan the underwater and then, feathers glistening with water-drops, paddle its black-webbed feet under the surface to catch up with the rest. How easy it seems, she thought, to swim along with the current, let the river decide direction, float and enjoy.

Reflections of sunset on the green water brightened shadows cast by willows and some scudding clouds which seemed to her to be fringed with blood. She stood up carefully, one hand protecting her belly where earlier something inside her had fluttered and nudged her thoughts with its life. 'Let it be a son,' she whispered, her thoughts veering away from the heartache waiting for her, the agony of the day to come when the seven year old child would be taken away, returned to her own kin to be brought up by them as proof that the bond of peace had worked. If it could work. As if it possibly could.

~

It was the eve of Godric's journey and people from the monastery and the village came to wish him God speed. Odel's elderly father made his slow and unsteady way across the fields to whisper what words he could remember of a journey charm told in his boyhood days: 'I surround myself in God's protection,' he muttered slowly, 'entrust myself to his keeping against the pain in the side, against the scourge of a serpent's sting, against the horror that all men fear, against terror in the land.'

Nerienda's gift was a piece of dried eel skin to ward off evil spirits. 'I know it's superstitious,' she said, 'but it may save you from harm.' Other sisters packed him a bag for the journey as well as one each for the two young monks who were also going. In the bag they put a fruit loaf, some walnuts, boiled eggs, dried apples, water and ginger wine. Hilde gave him lots of instructions and an extra warm woollen cloak.

That night, as a change from eel broth, the travellers enjoyed a special treat of hot kale and chestnut soup. Soon after twilight they were well prepared and ready for adventure.

~

Hilde's Fragment III

Now try this. Maybe that young woman, moody and pregnant, wasn't a peace-weaver, wasn't a princess. Perhaps she was merely a child of the Fens, daughter of a blacksmith or farmer or one who made salt. Was she cast out in disgrace from her home, left to bring up her infant of shame? Or could she have been a married woman, caught out in adultery, waiting for the vengeance of her kin? Truth, like the green river the girl is watching, is fluid, may be affected by something as slight as a swan's feather. Hers may become a song for a scop, a giedd of lamentation as she sits on a mound in the rain, weeping. Who knows? A good story must pass through many versions in its quest for the best one.

~

Lindisfarne – a dream-like setting ringed with visions or a place of horror? Either or both, few people can walk away unmoved.

'This sequestered nook of story,' Tacitus called the island. The author of the Saxon poem *The Ruin* talks about 'frost in the plaster.' He should have mentioned the spaces between, the echoes in thin cracks.

~

It was still dark when Godric and his companions dipped their toes in water at the start of the watery trudge along the Pilgrim's Way. Day after day of tedious, bone-rattling travel by horse and cart, catching sleep when he could at monastery or hostelry, had rather blurred the distinction between day and night for him, but the moonlight showed him miles of dark sand ahead and a very faint light on the horizon where Lindisfarne lay. Like the twenty or so other pilgrims waiting to cross to the island, Godric walked barefoot, his woollen robe tied securely round his waist, his pilgrim's staff in his hand. The guide nodded, the tide was low, the way across was safe. Godric, at the head of the band of pilgrims, stepped bravely into the sea.

The guide was confident and strode briskly through the water, following the line of cairns that gave clear markers along the route. Godric followed cautiously, nervous of slipping on seaweed, feeling his toes squelching in black mud. Tiny shells gritted underfoot and salt water stung his blisters and the sore patch on his ankle bone. One of the pilgrims began to play softly on his pipe and a couple of others were murmuring prayers. Step by step they splashed on, one foot in front of the other in a kind of trance. The island seemed very far away.

An hour or so later, although it felt much longer, Godric realised that for some time he had been listening to a low hum of sounds coming across the sea to the left of him. Moaning sounds, groans and the occasional bark. 'Seals,' said the guide when he enquired, 'Grey seals. They're everywhere here. You'll see them better from the shore.'

All around him now the sea was shimmering silver and red. The sand under his toes was a lighter brown and Godric could see the island not too far away with three monks waiting to greet the travellers and wash the grit from their feet. A cluster of ducks appeared from nowhere, bobbing around the group and forming a long line as if to lead them to land.

Godric felt his spirits lift with sudden joy. He had arrived where he longed to be and the brightening sky was his roof.

~

An exciting and a pleasing thing. The Priory on Lindisfarne, the original one Godric would have stepped into that first chilly morning of his visit, was not the same as those drenched-with-light ruins that tourists see today. The tale of those buildings belongs to a later date, is for others to recount. My pleasure lies in the fact that excavations of early medieval sites on Lindisfarne are beginning to reveal tiny Saxon clues.

Hints and glimpses. Geophysical surveys of fields around the present village suggest that possible locations of earlier sites, one to the east, one to the west, stretch over a larger area than the boundaries of the present ruins, lie deep beneath the modern shops and homes. There are other pointers – a small stone cross carved into a boulder, earthworks in an area known as the Heugh, stone remains of some long-houses and – most exciting – lots and lots of calf bones. How many skins went into the making of the Lindisfarne Gospels? 500 plus? Here, I feel, is proof that the early monastery made its own parchment, had its own thriving industry. This is what Godric has come to see.

Excavations take us back even further. Stone tools owned by Mesolithic hunters and gatherers, the earliest visitors to Lindisfarne, have been dug up, sifted, pieced together. These were people expert at recognising nature's rich resources, they would have caught the smell of herring and shellfish, fed themselves on seal meat and the flesh of winter gulls.

And here's another archaeological discovery. The early church was built on what seems to have been the most dangerous, wind-blown and rocky site that anyone could possibly discover. A few metres from the edge with the sea a sheer drop below. No wonder the spot was known as The Precipice. Why such a choice? Surely selected with much deliberation. To be closer to God? That's possible. As a lookout? Maybe. One fact I find enticing is that the building was made of gleaming white sandstone and visible from miles away. How beautiful and impressive it must have looked at dawn and at sunset or in the clear light of midday.

Another fact delights me. This white church surrounded by the wild sea was only four miles away from the royal palace of Bamburgh. Archaeologists say that nearby was a signalling tower, maybe twelve metres high with massively thick walls. How many beacon signals passed between them? What news was sent?

Bamburgh. A later castle now stands where the Northumbrian kings had lived. A castle like Camelot; legends claim the setting as Joyous Gard. A castle used countless times in film sets – it's said that if there's a medieval castle in a film it is most likely to be Bamburgh. And there are the golden sands where I shall always imagine Charlton Heston as El Cid in the film, dead but propped up as if still alive on his saddle, leading his army with thundering hooves across that magnificent beach.

~

Hilde's Fragment IV

Caput gerat lupinum (May he bear a Wolf's Head) was the sentence passed on outlaws and this story may turn out to concern such a one – a man in hiding, a man named Wulf in fear of his life in the Fens. Outlaw as animal. This is what the judgement implied – instant slaughter and a gutted carcass rotting and picked to the bone.

And the hunters? Blood-lust and the crushing of the vulnerable were crucial elements in predation's game.

How long could an outlaw be concealed? As long as an island's forests obliterated his shape; as long as his foot was steady, not sinking him up to his nostrils in swamp; as long as wolf and wild boar never caught the smell of his fear.

Now enter the villain. Every tale must have one otherwise we shall not recognise the hero when he comes peering through the gloom.

Let us call our villain Eadwacer. That may be an alias, one of many, but no matter. His role for today shall be that of husband though he is not the kind to cherish and protect a woman for he is one who owns the land and all that grows or moves on it is his. He is lord of the market, overseer of every coin, every bushel of bread or eel, each tear of his sad wife.

Proud cockerel. Think of him watching and waiting for sunrise so he may shatter human sleep and force his will upon his minion hens. See him crested and feathered in scarlet against a dreary sky. He is supreme.

Eadwacer. A bestial name to bring in shivers. Blood-spatters on lichen, there is a fester of guts. Words like flank, chine, offal, haunch, hang in the air like a hook on a slaughter-house door. No time now, young girl, for gazing at ducks and river sunsets. See how your pretty blue sky is mottled white, marbled in grease and fat.

~

Godric came to Lindisfarne as a pilgrim and there is still a strong sense of pilgrimage here in these acres of land and sea. Above all there is an impression of Cuthbert, the hermit-bishop who was loved and venerated. His mark is here, for all time.

Why is he remembered so well? Is it the Disney touch that endears, the eiderducks safe within his protection, the tale of two otters who dried his wet feet with their fur, blew warm breath on his cold face?

Maybe it is the ascetic side of him we admire, the hermit in surroundings so brutal and icy the thought alone makes us shiver.

Whatever, he is still here in the cries of guillemots and jackdaws, the underwater music of the grey seal each dawn and dusk.

Romantic images these, fit for illustration in a Child's Book of Saints. Yet something blurs this perfection for me – too many homespun bits of psychology in my head impede the vision, offer me a Cuthbert with feet (and maybe a whole trunk) of clay.

This is what comes of trying to separate man from myth. I have stood on the beach at Lindisfarne and looked across the narrow stretch of water to St Cuthbert's Isle, the scrap of land he cherished as a hermitage with its low rampart of black dolerite rock to ward off the waves, a simple wooden cross as marker. This I can understand. The Saxon equivalent of a room of one's own, the longing for peace and quiet and privacy. How frustrating it must have been to be followed out there by many acolytes, by those who regarded their quest for spiritual guidance to be more urgent than their mentor's need for solitude. Cuthbert must have dreaded the sound of water splashing beyond his wall as the faithful swam or waded joyfully towards him to receive his blessing and words of welcome – for he seems to have been always courteous and sweet of temper.

And I can well understand him finding this small patch of island too accessible and escaping to the Farne Islands, those bare and brutal rocks in the North Sea where he could be "more remote from mankind" as the chronicler says. It must have been soothing to the spirit to hear no voices except those of terns and razorbills, kittiwakes and puffins. A fine list of the self-sufficient.

But the way he immured himself in a cell in his zeal for perfection – building it with his own hands, stone by heavy stone, if we believe the accounts, leaving only a tiny window for air and light although "as time went on he shut even that" so that in the end "he could see nothing except the heavens above."

Salvation means different things to each of us. If, for Cuthbert and the young anchoress at Willingham, that involved the slow closing of earthly light in hope of a radiant heavenly one, that was their choice and they were steadfast.

One story amuses me. It tells how Cuthbert's "demons" were exorcised and banished by him to another island some distance away. Here witnesses claim to have seen them many times, short in stature with hideous faces, riding on black goats.

What a lot there is to say about a man dead two hundred years before my story even begins.

~

The day felt warm for mid-October and the sky over Lindisfarne was cloudless and blue. Godric cursed his bad luck at waking up with a heavy cold and scratchy throat. 'Just don't get too near my powders,' said Ambrose, the monk assigned to show Godric the buildings. 'One sneeze from you and they'll go everywhere.'

Godric gazed around, marvelling at the display of coloured powders and inks. Blues, purples, greens and yellows, reds in every shade from crimson to pale pink. He thought he had never seen such a display, each colour contained in its own small horn pot with all of them neatly arranged in their categories on long wooden shelves.

'You'd better tell me exactly what you need to know,' said Ambrose. 'I'm not sure how much progress you've made at Ely.'

'Not a great deal, I'm afraid. Not yet. Mother Hilde, our Abbess, is full of energy and plans to begin an ambitious programme of pulling down many of the buildings we live and work in and replacing them with stone. She has this dream of Ely becoming a centre of learning that people will flock to from all over the world for hundreds of years to come. At the moment though, my scriptorium is a wooden hut, manuscripts are stored in a cell below the crypt, I work with whatever materials we can make or the Abbess can scrounge from elsewhere – but we still have such a lot to do. How could we begin to achieve even one quarter of the wonderful things you do here? It's impossible.'

'Nothing's impossible, Brother Godric. That's lesson number one. But listen, these wonderful things, as you call them, are nothing compared to what it was like a hundred years ago.' Ambrose looked grim. 'I doubt if Lindisfarne will ever recover from the havoc and devastation those infernal raiders caused. May they rot in hell, every last man of them. Anyway, enough of that, these are just some of our inks. I assume your group has already gathered in huge supplies of oak galls for your blacks and browns?'

'Yes, lots of our villagers turned up and helped us on St Michael's feast day. We thought it would take a very long time since the women insisted on checking each one in case it housed a bad luck spider. Old fears and practices die hard in Ely.'

'As they do here. And your gardens? Your stores? How are you doing with them?'

'Well we grow a great number of things for medicines, of course, but nothing on the scale you have here.'

'It will happen. Just make use of everything God has given you. Your lands must be rich in his gifts. Send the village children out with their baskets to collect leaves, bark, lichen, roots, all sorts of berries – rowan, rose hip, blueberries, the brighter the better – crab apples of course, chopped up they help to make a wonderful deep red.' Ambrose paused for breath. 'What else? – turmeric, woad, as much ochre as you can dig up, beetle blood, chalk, soot – get your good sisters boiling and pounding, tell your Abbess to send for the masons and build yourselves some proper buildings, get organised and you'll be amazed at how much you'll achieve in a short time. Over here I have a few pots of precious gold powder. You can admire them from a distance but don't you dare sneeze.'

~

Ambrose was busy the next day and had little time to continue with the guided tour apart from a quick look at the building where quills and brushes were kept. These, like the inks, were neat and ordered, categorised according to size, weight, style and texture.

'Choose something,' he said. 'Take yourself a new quill as a gift. Goose is best. Flight feathers. Left wing or right? Which hand do you use? Have a couple if you like.'

He hurried off to deal with urgent monastic issues. Godric, still heavy-headed with his cold, was glad to be left to his own devices, pleased to have the chance of exploring the island for a couple of hours and exchanging a few words of conversation with anyone who felt like talking to him.

This turned out to be no problem, people being happy to leave off what they were doing and chat, several seeking him out for themselves. It seemed to be an accepted part of Lindisfarne's hospitality that all visitors, whether from Paris or Rome or a nearby local church, should be regaled with a full account of its history from ancient times to the present, with special emphasis and pride on its saints, relics and treasures.

At dusk, Godric walked on the headland, thinking about the tales he had heard. One theme was constant – that dreadful day, seventy-six years previously, when raiders from the north had come over the horizon like dragons of fire, slaying people on the beaches and on their farms, plundering and burning the monastery almost to the ground, dragging monks and children into the sea and holding them under the waves, sailing away again in triumph on their long ships with jewels and silver stacked high, blood on their hands and many young people, screaming and weeping, tied up as hostages to be sold as slaves in a frightening, alien land.

Some of the stories told to Godric were first hand. One very old man, bent almost double with pain in his back, remembered himself as a child on that day, hiding behind a pile of logs, ready to fall down and play dead if need be. Later on he'd found the body of his mother, her gown ripped to shreds and her throat cut. He'd never found his father, only the charred remains of the family home. His brother, he was told, was last seen fighting the man who was binding him with rope and dragging him onto a ship.

Those terrible events, thought Godric, were as real to everyone living on Lindisfarne as if they had only just happened. Most of them hadn't even been born that day but they had drunk in horrors with their mothers' milk. There was bitterness and anger, of course, and pain at all that had been lost, not only at that time but since, with many monks and farmers forsaking the place and moving further inland for safety. But there was also a sense of acceptance – or of resignation at least – a stoicism in the face of whatever destiny had marked out for them, together with faith in a God who had permitted it all as some sort of punishment for the evil they must have allowed to creep in. There was gratitude too, to the same God who had kept the shrine of their saint from being destroyed, who had preserved the pages, if not the jewelled cover, of their beautiful book of Gospels. And always, of course, there was underlying fear. Everyone on Lindisfarne knew it could happen again.

The last of the sunset was fading with clouds above the monastery fringed with deep orange as Godric walked slowly back along the path. His head ached and he was looking forward to resting it soon in his bed. One thought above others was nagging at him – anxiety for the place he knew as home, fear for the ones he loved. How safe were they? Edmund, the king of their region, had, a while back, made an uneasy peace with the Northmen – peace in exchange for horses – but how strong an agreement was that? Pilgrims to Ely's hostelry came with many tales of atrocities and sudden attacks. Exaggerated, perhaps, but still the worry was there. I wish I was home, thought Godric. I need to look after them. Whatever fate has in store for us, I want to be there.

~

I wrote this poem over several days one Easter from the vantage point of a desolate shingle beach across the water from Lindisfarne. If Godric had been able to see into the future, he too might have felt like this:

The Space Between

This is no frigid shoreline. Secretive, yes, but obsessive in surrender: a restless gift of shells and fossils, pebbles and small bones. Across the clouds the ancient gods still battle in dispute. Pagan in a copper sun the sky devours the light...

which would have poured in benediction
down upon those Saxons who in nightmares
of a long dark ship awoke to find it true.
Here on this April morning, grey-seal rocks
outstretch across the sand. There are no screams
or dagger-thrusts, no muffled cries of children
shoved beneath the waves, no flames and ash
no wild demented bell.

Images shift in the memory pool: painted faces in the sand dunes cursing at invading saints, a slaughtered goat upon the grasses, omens read as signs in entrails and in blood.

Harsh as rock on Lindisfarne are cities in this hostile land
where those who journey with some hope discover
not a hand to hold and no proverbial inn.
Sleep is a shelter in the rain, food a discard bin.
Industrial skylines darken like a stone.

Across the sea the island sings with early birds who feast on particles washed up by waves and relish snails and tiny shrimps, engrossed for hours within the joy of digging.

This was the backcloth of the Priory once: herring, seaweed,
sugar and figs. Peer through cracks in a broken wall and you'll
smell hot bread and honey-mead, take note of Cuthbert, hermit-man,
beneath his stars.

He would have hated city streets with many strangers desperate for words. Summoned back to busy life he sickened and returned to solitude, his sanctuary...

as this beach is called a sanctuary for birds.
There's waterfowl of every kind, but are they safe
or are they under threat?

In bitter winds the greylag goose is culled;
there is no place on this bleak mudflat
for excess of bird.

How many are the ways to kill a dream? With guns and knives and hammer blows, an on/off switch on phone or keypad, someone's documents mislaid beneath a pile?

The priory on this island is a shell.
Dissolution is too soft a word for plunder and destruction.
The deletion of a name is just as quiet.

On Farne the kittiwakes make nests on sheerest rock –
for some there is no ledge, no hold, no room.

The space between the traffic lights thins to a winter chill.

In this place of dereliction, words are faint on graveyard stone:
Contra vim mortis, non est medicamen in hortis.
'Against the power of death there is no remedy in the garden.'

~

'Tell me about your Abbess,' said Ambrose the next morning as they walked towards one of several buildings devoted to the making of parchment. 'She is well known here, by repute. Only last year we had a visiting scholar from Paris whose father knew her in younger days when she was studying abroad. Is she as forceful as she sounds? People comment on how strong-willed and confident she appears.'

'Forceful and strong-willed, certainly,' said Godric. 'But I don't know about the confidence. There's something in her nature that drives her on and she never gives up until she achieves whatever she has set out to do. But sure of herself? I've known her for the best part of my life and, though she hides her feelings, she has a gentle side.'

'Well she is certainly making a name for the Abbey.' Ambrose sounded envious. 'Of course she is of royal blood and can afford to spend richly. We could do with some of that wealth here at Lindisfarne. I only hope she has made wise provision for the future since they say she has no daughter or niece to take up the role of Abbess when she dies.'

'I don't know,' said Godric slowly. 'I hadn't given any thought to that. As far as I can tell she has no offspring to continue the line. She never talks about her early life, apart from her time in the convent at Chelles where, apparently, she was recognised as a fine story teller.'

Ambrose chose one of the keys from the great bunch on his belt and unlocked the heavy door. Inside, facing them, were twenty or so circular frames with a variety of animal skins stretched tightly over them. Ambrose, peering closely at one, tutted with annoyance.

'This isn't good enough. Far too many hairs. It'll have to be scraped again.'

'What sort of skins are they?' Godric moved closer to the frames. 'Why are some white and some brownish?'

'Depends on the animal of course. White skin from white cattle, those with shadowy brown patterns are obviously from a brindled cow. Or a piebald goat.'

'I've never seen anything like it. You'll have to excuse me, Brother Ambrose, if I ask stupid questions, but this is the first time I've seen parchment in its raw state.'

Ambrose laughed. 'Raw state? I'll show you raw before you've finished here.'

'What's that smell? It's making my eyes sting.'

'Probably lime. There'll be up to a dozen skins at a time soaking in those vats over there. Vicious stuff but it's the only way to loosen hair and wool as well as killing off all the lice and beetle grubs. Give some of those insects half a chance and they'll munch their way through a manuscript in no time at all.'

~

Hilde's Fragment V

Wolves in the moonlight prowl silently in the shadow lands of this tale. Both real and myth, a wolf will gnaw at the edges of man's imagination for it is the wilderness itself. Guardian of its own boundaries, it will wait.

~

In St Cuthbert's church there were still many signs of the frenzied assault it had endured during the raid. The area round the altar, in particular, had suffered damage by fire. Nevertheless, the saint's oak carved coffin, now covered with a white linen cloth, remained intact and next to it, in a pale silver chest, were the intricate and finely detailed pages of Lindisfarne's precious book.

Godric had wondered if he was ever going to see this treasure. Everyone he had spoken to on the island said 'You must see the Gospels. Don't go back before you've seen the Gospels. Have you heard about our book?' He had also been regaled more times than he could remember by anecdotes passed down from father to son about the way it had all begun – how Eadfrith the monk had sat in his cold, gloomy scriptorium for month after month, laboriously but perfectly copying the words; how the purpose of the Gospels was not only to enshrine the words of Christ but also to honour St Cuthbert through them; how the magnificent book was intended to be shown, read and celebrated on the special day set for the saint's Elevation when his body, eleven years after his death on the Farne Islands, would be transferred from its stone sarcophagus to a new tomb by the high altar. At this point, as people recounted the story to Godric, their eyes shone and voices grew hushed with awe. 'It was a miracle,' they said. 'A God-given miracle. You'd expect there to be nothing but saintly bones and dust but inside the coffin the body was as fresh as on the day of death. Shining and uncorrupt. A miracle.'

Ambrose's voice was equally hushed and his hands were trembling as he took the book out of the chest and placed it carefully on a low table. 'Don't you touch it,' he instructed Godric. 'I'll turn the pages and tell you more about them.'

'Please don't turn them too quickly, Brother Ambrose. You can see this magnificent treasure any time but this is the one and only chance I shall ever get. I must take my impressions home to our Mother Abbess and the community. I need to remember everything.'

~

Later that evening, as he took his usual walk along the headland, Godric didn't know how he was ever going to sort out the jumble of images and motifs in his head, let alone describe them to others. Spirals, scrolls, whorls and vines, wild flying birds and fantastic leaping creatures interlaced and danced in front of his eyes in colours he had not realised a palette could produce – vivid, shining colours such as he had never seen, even in his dreams.

There was one image in the Gospels he had felt especially close to and that was the picture of St Luke the Evangelist. He was drawn to the curly-headed look of him, the way his feet were comfortable on a cushioned stool as he sat there day-dreaming, his hand poised to write on the long scroll unfurling on his lap. He had liked the calf with blue wings that flew above the gold halo on St Luke's head. The calf had a halo too, a smaller one. It made him think of his own monastery back in Ely where medallions of the Calf with Trumpet were made and sold to pilgrims as a symbol of sacrifice – Christ's sacrifice on the Cross. This in turn reminded him of Ambrose's words when they had parted earlier. 'Fifteen score of calf skins they say those Gospels took. Tomorrow, Godric my friend, you and I shall talk about vellum.'

~

When the morning came, however, Ambrose was in no great hurry to discuss the preparation of calf skin or visit the long building which was the vellum centre where the measuring, pricking, ruling and folding of parchments took place. 'First,' he said, 'we shall have another look at the inks since you are so interested in them.'

With instructions to keep their distance, and not even to breathe, they watched a scribe applying a delicate piece of gold leaf to a manuscript, burnishing it carefully with a dog's tooth. In another room several monks, working as scrapers, heaved piles of goatskins out of a vat where they had been soaking for days in lime and urine. Godric, trying to overcome the feeling of nausea induced by the smell of lime and the stench of bloody, meaty water, watched closely. He hadn't realised that the process involved a scraper holding a skin tightly against his own body while he attacked any leftover bits of flesh and gristle with a series of sharp knives. 'Well, you could lay the skin out on the floor or on a table,' said Ambrose, 'but these men find top to bottom scraping works better. They can always have a good sluice down at the end of the day. I'll get you a bag of parchment off-cuts to take home with you, if you like, to practise on. Maybe a few bits of vellum too, if there are any going spare.'

The vellum building comprised a series of low rooms, almost cellar like in their stone walls and lack of daylight. 'You'll note that nothing is ever wasted here,' said Ambrose. 'We pride ourselves on using every bit of carcass. Since the farmers work so well with the monastery in supplying a ready stock of calves all year round, the least we can do is give them good batches of meat in return.'

Godric, rather nervously, peered into a huge barrel. 'Horns,' said Ambrose. 'Perfect for inkwells after they've been boiled and cored. I'll get you a couple. One of our monks makes a point of using samples of left-over horn to make tiny spoons for visitors to buy. You can take a few of them as well.'

'What's in this barrel?' said Godric, moving down the line. 'Hooves?'

'Right. Great for glue. There's probably a couple of heads in that one over there – essential for glue as well and brains make excellent grease. The other barrels are probably full of bones. They're useful for all sorts of things – compost of course and small items such as combs and pins that the farmers' women like.'

Godric felt his head spinning with all the information. Could Ely, on a smaller scale, ever be as organised as this? It would, of course, mean more paid work for the villagers and they might well be glad of that in the hungry months of winter.

'And here,' said Ambrose, 'we have the skinning room. You're in luck, Brother. Some new calves, born and slaughtered yesterday, just brought in.'

Godric, taking a deep breath, stared at a calf hanging upside down on a hook. Someone had already cut off the hooves and washed the carcass to get rid of blood and dung. One of the butchers, knife in hand, made a quick cut in one foot, sliced up the leg and around the anus, hacked swiftly through the other leg and slid the whole skin down as easily as if slipping of a robe.

'Good, isn't he?' said Ambrose. 'He and the others compete sometimes to see who can be the fastest skinner. Godric, my friend, you're looking a bit green. Don't tell me you haven't got the stomach for butchery. I think you must live a life of luxury at Ely.'

~

Sunrise, two days later, saw Godric wandering along the beach, idly picking up pebbles and shells, peering into rock pools in the company of curlews and gulls. Shivering in the bitter cold, he tugged his woollen cloak tightly around him, hoping for a warmer day ahead for the start of his long journey home. His travel bag would be heavier than when he had arrived. Ambrose, possibly wanting to make up for his sarcastic remarks about Godric's easy life, had given him three rolls of parchment, several off-cuts of the finest vellum, countless tiny pots of coloured powders, goose feather quills of different sizes, a set of knives, pieces of chalk, two pumice stones, a new wax tablet and stylus – Godric could hardly wait to begin.

He thought about the way he had reacted to the skinning of the calf. Ambrose was right about the queasiness he'd felt. He wondered why it should be so. Surrounded by livestock most of his life, the sights and sounds of butchery were nothing new. There'd be killing enough in Ely fields in the coming month, the slaughter month they called November. It was either that or starve. It was something about the calf hanging there that had affected him: only just born the calf was just as soon dead. Unbidden, some words came into his head – *An enemy took my life* – no, that wasn't right, *took* wasn't strong enough – *An enemy robbed me of my life* – that was better – *An enemy robbed me of my life, pillaged my strength* – yes, the words were coming now – *they plunged me in water, soaked me, then heaved me out and set me to dry in the sun.*

He repeated the phrases several times to himself to memorise them. It would be many days before he'd have chance to write them down. A flight of wild geese overhead startled him with their flapping wings and their abrasive, high pitched screams.

Godric shivered again. The whole coastline seemed to be moaning now in the rough wind. A cormorant with its wings outstretched sat brooding on a rock, unflinching and motionless. Was this, he wondered, how Eadfrith had gained the inspiration for his illuminations, his symbols and motifs? By musing, dreaming, quiet as a cormorant, letting his imagination fill?

A feather was floating in a pool. Godric picked it up and dried it on his cloak. Too ragged to make a quill it would be a keepsake of his walk and his poem about the calf. *The bird's joy* – yes, he must bring in that phrase as well. He might find the poem turned into a riddle, in which case he could add it to his collection.

With the sky quiet and the horizon lit by the sun, Godric turned inland. It was time to go.

~

A digression while the monks from Ely make their long way home.

Godric, I imagine, will, as always, be keeping himself to himself, impervious to puddles and ruts in the tracks, not always answering his fellow travellers if they speak to him for he is in a world of his own, frequently unaware that anyone else is there.

We know very little about him. He is mentioned once, briefly, in the fragment of a document discovered two centuries ago at Lindisfarne. Whether this was Ambrose's work, maybe part of a fuller description of his visitor from Ely, we shall probably never know. On parchment he is described as a man of intelligence and middle years. In my mind's eye I see him as tall and slender, in his late thirties or early forties, pale of complexion with thin fair hair. I cannot see the colour of his eyes for he, as usual, is gazing at the ground, deep in thought, his shoulders hunched.

I feel there is a kind of absence about Godric which is more than introversion. Something empty and unfulfilled in the heart of him. Is it a sense of personal identity that is missing? He seems to have suffered a form of amnesia in his earlier years. The time before the monastery seems to him now like an un-scribed tablet, his few memories are shadowy and blurred. He thinks he remembers being brought to the monastery by two men but has no recollection of who they were, how old he was, or for what purpose he was taken. He remembers Hilde greeting him that day with warmth and welcome and a look on her face that struck him as something close to love. He remembers hours of instruction in the Christian faith and the monastic life. He remembers his vows and the quiet years since.

Before that, nothing. Only an impression of loss. Sometimes he imagines himself as a bird, one who has fallen wingless from a high tree, a being of earth but even more so of air.

This sense of loss, this longing to re-capture the missing years, is always with him but slowly, very slowly, it is beginning to grow less, the gap closing with every morsel of knowledge he learns, every psalm he scribes, every new story he hears.

~

And the others in our tale? What have they been doing during this space of time? How far along their own roads have they journeyed?

Hilde, I expect, is as busy as ever making arrangements for the christening and ceremonial raising of the bell. She will be waiting anxiously for Godric's safe return, longing to begin her scheme of establishing a fine scriptorium at Ely under his guidance, seeing the double monastery become a centre of learning in her own lifetime. She prays every day that this may be so and that, God willing, she will be spared a few more years.

And Nerienda? What of this conflicted young woman whose vocation for the religious life has begun to fall apart over the last few months? Will she now, if given half a chance, renounce her faith, scandalise the community and run, lovesick, to Odel? He, at the moment, has other worries of his own – an aged and increasingly ailing father together with seven hungry younger siblings dependant on him to provide.

And Asmund, where is he? Rumours suggest, alarmingly, that the Great Army is slowly moving its men out of York and into East Anglia itself, closer to Thetford where King Edmund has his stronghold. Is Asmund there, one among many? Or is it possible that he is one of the few chosen for the role of spy and is now searching for hidden paths to monasteries and priories, checking out places of affluence, snouting, pig-like, for wealth? Maybe, even now, he waits: a hooded sleuth in the darkness of Ely's woods.

And it's into this deep darkness that the travellers return. What will they see as they stumble wearily along the track? Any rush-lights still quivering in cell or hovel will be dimmer than a firefly in the woods. Candles inside the Abbey will, as always, be lit, a dozen or more of them around St Etheldreda's shrine flickering in the glow. Here Godric and the others must, at the moment of arrival, prostrate themselves before the altar and ask everyone to pray for them, begging forgiveness for faults committed by them on their travels including idle chatter or dozing too long in bed. Most important of all, they must implore divine protection for themselves and the whole community from foul fiends and evil spirits that may have crept behind them all the way from Lindisfarne and now lurk in the gloom.

~

Odel's father was sick. He had been unwell and close to death in May at the time of the incident with the swarm of bees but his health had improved and he had rallied enough to make his slow way across the fields to give Godric the blessings of a journey charm before the party set out for Lindisfarne. Now, however, he was ailing again, the pain in his aching legs matched by fever and swellings in his upper limbs and face. 'His breathing is dreadful, Mother Abbess,' said Odel. 'You can hear every breath gasp in his throat. It's agony for him to suffer like this and for us to witness. The rash on his face is terrible to see. There are pustules oozing all across his forehead and his eyes are like slits.'

'I have seen plenty worse.' Hilde was busy making up a basket of salves and lotions. 'Sisters, don't stand around idle. There is a hungry brood in Odel's house and a mother at her wit's end. We have plenty to spare. Odel, we will be with you before noon. Sister Nerienda, see how many blankets you can find. A feverish man could die without warmth in this freezing weather.'

The small room where the sick man lay was thronged with people anxious to help. Odel's mother was sobbing in a corner as her daughters fluttered round her, dabbing their eyes and muttering words of comfort. Only the youngest girl seemed to have any sense of purpose as she stood next to the pallet holding a bucket of water.

'This man needs air.' The crowd round the bed moved aside respectfully to let Hilde in. 'Odel,' she continued, 'there are too many people starving this man of breath. It will be best if those who are not family wait outside.'

Several villagers left the hut, muttering among themselves. Three remained, huddled close to the door.

'We're losing him,' said Odel, feeling the sick man's failing pulse. 'He's drenched in sweat and shivering. There's nothing anyone can do.'

'Nonsense,' said Hilde. 'You give up too easily. With the help of Christian prayer and my potions we shall try. Poor man, his eyes look so hot and swollen. The sisters have brought a special pot of garlic and leek steeped in wine. That will ease the swelling and reduce the fever. Sister Nerienda, stroke the lotion carefully over his eyelids with a feather, not getting it in his eyes of course but all the way round them and on the skin underneath.'

'I've got the crab here.' Odel's little sister held out the bucket.

Hilde peered inside. 'Well you can certainly make him some nourishing broth from that if you kill it and prepare the meat carefully. Do you need the sisters to help you?'

The child looked horrified. 'It's not to eat! Not yet anyway. If we gouge its eyes out and place them on my poor father's eyes, the swelling will go down. Everyone knows that.'

'Everyone except me, obviously. I think I will use my own lotions. I would rather not be involved in any gouging out today though it is clever of you to discover such a remedy. Go and put some sticks on the fire and see how good you are at cooking some lunch for your mother. Odel, I need you to boil some water so we can make an infusion from dried wenwort. Nerienda, you may help him.'

An hour later Hilde, having said prayers for the sick, was ready to leave. 'He looks a bit better,' said Odel. 'I think all your medicines are bringing the fever down.'

'We shall pray for him, day and night. I think he should rest now. Keep him warm and do not let him be overtired with visitors. Odel, why are those men still here? What are they waiting for? What are they holding?'

Odel glanced at the three men who were whispering among themselves. 'I think they are waiting for you to go so they can try out their own remedies on my father and recite their own charms to cure him. They hold magic tokens in that leaf that will reduce the swellings on his face.'

'What tokens? There is no need for magic and superstition here. Odel, you know that.'

'The old beliefs are still important to them, Mother Abbess. Those tokens will have been gathered and treasured by their fathers and grandfathers.'

Odel's mother came over to them. 'I cannot thank you and the sisters enough, Mother Abbess. Blessings on you all. The fever is breaking, I think. My husband may live to see another day.'

'With God's blessing he will yet celebrate another Yule or two with us.' Hilde smiled at the woman. 'You have a fine family and it gives me pleasure to see the love between you all.'

'A fine family indeed though at times I could wish there were less of us. It is a heavy burden for Odel with seven sisters hanging on his heels.'

'They will be gone sooner than you know it, bringing their strong husbands to help with the farm and a brood of grandchildren for you to spoil.'

'I pray it may be so. I hope that Odel may soon find himself a wife who will share the work of the household with me. I have seen many pretty girls cast an eye at him, you know, but so far he will have none of them.' She lowered her voice. 'He says there is only one he would have for a wife but the situation is impossible and they can never be together. He won't tell me what the matter is. God forbid a married woman is enticing him out of his wits!'

'There are some who love deeply and yet their union may never happen in this world.' Hilde picked up her basket of lotions. 'You can go and use your magic now,' she said to the group of men as she walked past. 'I would rather your words were those of prayer but if your charms are recited with love and good intention, then who am I to deny them.'

She paused outside the door. 'Sisters, what exactly are those tokens?'

'An eagle's feather and the claw of a wolf,' said Nerienda promptly. 'Odel told me.'

The voices of the men reciting their charm followed the group as they walked slowly across the fields. A few flakes of snow were falling and the sky was white. The words echoed in Hilde's head:

Under the wolf's foot, under the eagle's wing,
Under the wolf's claw, grow into nothingness.
May you become as small as a linseed grain,
Much less than the bone of an itchworm,
Shrivel smaller and smaller until you are gone.

~

Hilde's Fragment VI

It was a cold, hard, white world when the young woman in our tale gave birth to a boy. Images of that evening are blurred like the spoor of a wild animal covered over by snow and events come down to us as distorted and warped. There are rags, blood-red and soaking wet; there are screams of pain and tears – so many tears; there is a voice, strident and harsh issuing orders and there is something ...

~

'No,' said Hilde. 'I will not postpone the ceremony. The bishop has come all this way in the worst of weathers and others have spent many hours in preparation for this day. We are none of us so feeble-minded and timid, I hope, as to be troubled by a few snowflakes. Now let us all go outside and play our part in the dedication of this beautiful bell.'

Outside, Hilde's few flakes had turned into a downpour of snow and the bell, dressed in a thin-white christening veil, was scarcely visible on its low platform. The bishop, also in white, shivered and his teeth chattered as he un-wrapped the necessary salt and holy water, ready to begin the service of exorcism. Around him, the forty monks and nuns of the community stood patiently, dripping wet and frozen cold but stoical and devout.

'God's creature, Salt,' began the bishop. 'I cast out the demon from you by the power granted to me by the living God. May you be a purified salt, a means of health for body and soul. May all evil fancies of the foul fiend, his malice and cunning, be driven from the place where you are sprinkled.'

Nerienda, on the edge of the group, closed her eyes and lifted up her face to the falling snow. As if from a distance she heard the bishop exorcising the holy water, empowering it against evil influences of the air and against fallen angels and lurking devils. Her eyelashes, already wet with earlier tears, now dripped with snow.

'Praise the Lord,' intoned the nuns who had been practising for hours. Their voices sounded thin in the snow-heavy air. 'Let every breath praise Him from deep mountains and all hills, fruitful trees and all cedars, beasts and all cattle, creeping things and feathered birds.'

Hilde, who seemed impervious to the weather although her thin gown was soaked, lifted the wet veil off the bell which shone in its bronze newness in the white light. The bishop, pouring salt in the shape of the cross into the water, began the naming: 'Through Our Lord Jesus Christ you shall be called by the name of Felix. May the faithful servants of our holy Master hear the voice of your peal and be strengthened in piety and faith, opposing all slanders of the devil. May storms, hail, whirlwinds, fearful thunder and lightning, evil and destructive winds be calmed and made to cease at your joyful ringing.'

At these words the sky was seared by streaks of lightning and the thunder, which had been rumbling beyond the distant fields, crashed over the heads of the little group as if the heavens themselves were exploding.

'It's an omen,' whispered Nerienda.

The bishop, hurrying his actions, anointed the bell. 'By the sprinkling of this Holy Water,' he said, his words scarcely audible above the thunder, 'this bell is blessed and sanctified in the Name of the Father, of the Son, and of the Holy Spirit.'

'Amen,' muttered the bedraggled group, beginning to move away.

'Wait!' cried Hilde. 'We cannot leave it like this. The bell has been christened, it has a name, it must be raised to the top of the Abbey tower and our two bells must ring out together. Everything has been performed with this in mind. We have all been planning this moment for months. We cannot just leave it!'

'It's impossible, Mother Abbess,' said the man in charge of the pulleys. 'Absolutely out of the question. Look how icy the ground is! We'd slide and break our necks. Far too dangerous to try. In any case the ropes are unlikely to hold. They are already too slippery and heavy. Even if we got halfway the bell might come crashing down on our heads before we could raise it further and fix it safely in place.'

'Then we must leave it in God's hands for another day.' Hilde was a small white blur on the snow covered lawn. 'It shall be whatever he intends. His decision, not ours. We must hope and pray that nothing else begins to fall apart.'

The sky was lit up as if by streaks of silver fire as everyone scurried indoors. Only Nerienda remained outside, excited by the turbulence and relishing the storm.

~

Fragment VII *Hilde's last surviving fragment*

... there is something wolf-cub small being wrapped in a cloth and carried out of the door.

Fragments of this story are beginning to un-weave. Outside the room where the woman sleeps, the landscape is thickly covered in snow that is white and featureless as death. Inside, the rush-light is dim. The woman on the bed is exhausted, worn out by her ordeal and by hours of weeping. She stirs, reaches out for a baby that is now missing, reaches out again as if to touch her lover who she hasn't seen or held for such a long time and, most probably, will never see again. 'Wulf,' she whispers. 'My Wulf.'

~

And there all references to this baby appear to end. Was it taken away to be abandoned in the forest, left to die in the bitter night air, a prey for ravenous wild beasts? Was this its fate as an unwanted child of shame? Or was it smuggled away, to be cared for by a wet-nurse and fostered by a local couple in exchange for gold? Or was it taken abroad to join its mother's kin, a peace-weaver's token of faith? Or was this child, incredibly, somehow rescued by Wulf, that enigmatic figure who is both hunted and loved?

~

'It worked before.' Godric paused on his way to the hiding place in the cellar where his latest manuscripts were being stored. 'They were content enough in those days with the King's offer of horses and provisions for the winter.'

'Their army was smaller then and poorly organised.' Hilde was watching a long line of people trudging across the fields towards the Abbey. 'Godric, this worries me – so many bags and boxes being left in nooks and crannies all over the place and everyone trusting us to keep them safe in case of attack. There are more and more people turning up every day!'

'Many are coming from Soham, I think. I've heard the Abbot there is refusing to store any more belongings.'

'How unkind of him. I will gladly offer storage to any man's small treasures. My concern is how to keep them protected. Stone is safer than wood, I'll grant you that, Godric, but against a plundering army, I don't know. Men say that Thetford is overflowing with armed and brutal soldiers who long for a fight. Who will hold them back if their minds are set on war? I tremble for my little flock, Godric. We are lambs to their wolf.'

'Well, they say King Edmund is a shrewd man so we must look to him to make the best terms for peace in our land. We must pray he has the strength and skill to take this shadow from us.'

~

Now I must leave my characters to cope with this shadow alone for I cannot intervene and no words of mine will change the destiny that is beginning to unfold around them. They belong to their own lives and they must live them.

~

As the blood-month days of November were drawing to a close a mood of darkness, much thicker and heavier than any marsh fog, settled over the fields of Ely and sank into the thoughts of men.

Most of the snow was beginning to melt except for several boulders of tightly-packed muddy ice by the north wall of the Abbey, a hazard to anyone hurrying along that way at dusk. Sister Alfryd, the oldest nun in the community, who had trouble finding her way on even the brightest of mornings, stumbled and gashed her shin on one of them leaving a wound that was still bleeding days later.

At this time many weird and disturbing events occurred, leading the superstitious to mutter about witchcraft and dark elves. The bell, still earth-bound on its platform, was discovered early one morning swathed in holly from which all red berries had been stripped. There was a nest in the middle of this garland and in it lay a dead wren.

Were people so terrified of what the coming weeks might have in store for them that they would symbolically hasten the demise of winter and the Holly King? Hilde, knowing all the ancient tales, guessed this was so. 'The sun won't be re-born until it decides it is ready,' she said to Nerienda as they buried the bird. 'No amount of sacrifice will speed this year on its way. This is the low time and we have no choice but to live with it.' She patted down the earth over the wren's small grave.

Odel reported even more problems and sinister happenings. 'No one will help me to cut the reeds back so we can make safe tracks across the marsh and they are all avoiding the woods saying they are cursed by flickering lights small as gnats or sometimes big as a ball. These are tormented spirits they claim, wraiths from out of purgatory who would lead us falsely into the swamp and snatch our souls away. Mother Hilde, I've seen these lights myself, many times.' Odel's voice was shaking. 'Last week I buried one knife by the river and another at the edge of the forest to sever this world from that of the dead. But it's no good. The spirits of unburied corpses are coming back to take their revenge and haunt us in every tree and every pool of water. Many people now are digging deep holes outside their huts and burying bones left over from the slaughter as offerings to any being that will keep them from harm. Yesterday I found a pig's head in the mud with its snout facing down towards the under-earth. We are in terrible danger, Mother. Surely you can feel it!'

~

After the incident with the wren and the holly, Hilde made a priority of raising the new bell to the Abbey tower. This proved to be a dismal affair, an anti-climax after the ceremony of its baptism in a snowstorm. The community of nuns and monks was there of course but most of the villagers stayed away, regarding the previous lack of success as a curse of ill-luck and the tempest as a message of doom.

Slowly, with the aid of a pulley and six strong men, the bell was heaved skywards into its place. Stark in outline against the grey clouds it shone for one bright moment in its bronzeness. There was no peal. 'Best if we wait for a week or two until Yuletide,' said Hilde to the group. 'Then the two bells in unison shall ring out in joy and celebration, all morning long if we like. Everyone for miles around shall hear the song of our two bells and be glad.'

~

Later that same evening, Sister Alfryd was carried into the infirmary after suffering another fall on hard ground. In the short time it took Hilde to rush to her side, the nun was feverish and babbling words that made no sense. Ten minutes later she died. Nerienda, kneeling at her bedside, was distraught, weeping as if her heart would break, for the old woman had been very close to her, listening with sympathy to the confidences of the young novice but offering no judgement on anything she heard.

Hilde turned angrily on a cluster of nuns who were whispering about the curse of the bell. 'Leave your idle and ridiculous talk,' she snapped. 'We have just lost a rare and precious sister. We shall not find her kind again. Save your foolish breath and pray that together with God's holy angels she may find her due reward in heaven where she shall rest eternally in peace. May she in her saintliness pray for us who are left, who now without her goodness still suffer on this earth.'

~

'Sister Nerienda, what do you think you are doing?'

Hilde walked slowly towards the novice who she had been watching for several minutes. The girl, thinking herself unobserved, had been kneeling in prayer by the newly-dug grave of Sister Alfryd but then had reached into the pocket of her gown and taken out some objects which she buried in wet earth by the graveside, scrabbling with her fingernails to make a deep hole. Completing this she stood up, bowed in the direction of the grave and then walked steadily backwards.

'Oh, you startled me, Mother,' said the girl, looking guilty. 'I was just praying for the soul of our dear sister.'

'And what items did you bury a moment ago? Tell me the truth.'

'Nothing but a few crab apples and some hazelnuts.' Nerienda's eyes were bright with tears. 'I cannot bear to think of her in the cold earth so comfortless. Hazelnuts were her special favourite.'

'But foolish child, she is in God's hands now. She has no need of earthly food or comforts. What can you be thinking?'

'I am so sorry, mother.'

'But what are you sorry for? That you have angered and upset me? That you are failing in your Christian faith, in your duty to trust Our Lord to take care of our sister in heaven? This is superstition. Superstitious and dangerous nonsense! These apples and nuts are no better than grave goods. Grave goods! I prayed such wild beliefs were long since forgotten.'

'Mother, I really am so sorry. It won't ever happen again.'

'And why were you walking backwards? I was watching. You walked backwards as if it was a ritual, some secret ceremony.'

Nerienda burst into tears. 'It will stop her returning to this unhappy world. Actions in reverse will separate the dead and their realm from our living one. Odel's father told me!'

'Child, you horrify me. How could the spirit of our gentle sister in Christ ever come back to haunt us or do us harm. I think you have lost your wits as well as your faith!'

'I know her spirit would never want to hurt or frighten us. But I am so afraid she might be forced to return, to warn me and punish me for my terrible neglect.'

'Neglect? You may have neglected your faith but never the love and care you showed for Sister Alfryd. You were always there when she needed an arm to lean on or to show her the path on a dark night.'

Nerienda took a breath. 'No. Not that. It was last Yule. I left the holly for too long in the church – not all of it but two sprigs with the brightest berries. I thought nothing so beautiful could possibly bring us harm. I hid them in a tiny nook behind the shrine of our blessed saint. The other sisters would have been terrified at the thought of bad luck but they didn't see me. Now my wickedness has brought evil upon us all!'

'Sister, I am completely lost for words. Are you saying that the holly bush is the cause of all our recent troubles? I hope it was not you – Nerienda, tell me you were not the one who put that dead wren in the bell!'

'Never! I love all God's birds. I would never hurt a feather of one.'

'We must talk again. Not now. Your words trouble me greatly. Dear Sister, we must heal your soul and clear away all these doubts and confusions. I have been hoping for many months that you will soon be ready to make your vows. Maybe at Yuletide or not long after? I shall make arrangements to bring your father and your brothers from Stuntney to share in the occasion. We shall have the finest celebration afterwards with great ringing peals of our Felix bell so that all men shall know it brings no ill luck but only joy.'

'Mother ... I must talk to you. Mother, I cannot ...'

'Not now, my child. You must not speak hastily. Dry your eyes. We shall talk on a happier day.'

~

The next days brought little chance of happiness to anyone. Maybe Odel's sister and her friends played merry games of hide and seek around the village square but for the adults the threat of needing a real place to hide in felt only too real. Hilde, in the few hours of rest available to her, abandoned the idea of sleep altogether, her nerves taut with stress and her brain churning with plans.

Rumours had never been so rife. Travellers arrived on foot or by raft, haggard and anxious and barely stopping for a bowl of soup on their way to safety, wherever that might be. Some brought hopeful news: 'Talks are going well. They say the king is confident he'll get us a lasting peace.' Others muttered of doom and gloom: 'The king is on the run. Every path in Thetford is streaming with blood. They're stringing them up in the forest, little children too!'

'We must start to move people out,' said Hilde during one of her frequent talks with Odel. 'Those who are strong must pack a few simple things for the family, take water and some salted meat for the journey and begin to travel south or anywhere far away from this deadly army. One day, pray God, they may be able to return.'

'My father and mother and all the girls?' Odel chewed his nails already bitten down to the quick. 'My father cannot walk more than a few steps and a gust of wind will blow him straight off his feet.'

'They must, of course, have the horse and cart. Two of my most able monks shall go with them and make good provision for their safety and health. But Odel, I am afraid I cannot spare you. I need you here.'

The young man nodded slowly. 'I understand. I have given you my word.'

'And as for my sisters and brothers in Christ, I must consider where may be best for them to find sanctuary until these dark days pass. Soham is too near, close to danger as we are. Maybe the Abbey at Peterborough or someplace further west.'

~

The exodus from the village began, though less rapidly than Hilde had hoped. Many, especially the older people, refused to leave their farms and dwellings, preferring to take their chances. 'The king will see us safe,' said one. 'The Lord will watch over us,' said another. 'If we are to have our throats cut, then so be it, that is our fate,' said a third. Several nodded their heads.

Odel, searching for Hilde, found her in the Abbey church, kneeling by St Etheldreda's shrine. 'Bad news,' he said. 'There's no sign of the horse and cart. Someone has made his own escape with them.'

'That is worrying.' Hilde rose slowly to her feet. The shrine, glowing with its gold and candles, cast a soft light on her face, a shimmer round her head. 'We have other horses. Stable one securely in your name and see how quickly you can build another cart. No, on second thoughts, that will take too long – a litter for your father perhaps, or some sort of sledge. Get some of the brothers to help you. Tell them it is my wish. Here comes Godric – I could offer you his services but I doubt if he would know how to knock two pieces of wood together. He would, I fear, be more hazard than help.'

~

The following November morning seemed extra dark with no sign of dawn, but everyone in the monastery had already been up for hours. Rushlights all around the village flickered in doorways as people packed, wept, hugged each other, prepared to leave.

Godric, ordered by Hilde to make sure all his parchments, tablets, pens and inks were safely stored in the cellar below the crypt, heaved as many stones as he could to block the entrance. Odel, who had been working all night on the litter, wiped the sweat off his face and gave a sigh of relief. Nerienda, running between kitchen and dormitory, urged all the nuns to hurry with their preparations and gather together in the church, ready to be on the move.

This last part of the plan led to angry words between Hilde and the young girl.

'What do you mean, you are not going? I am relying on you, Sister Nerienda, to be at the head of the group. You must be the leader!'

'There are others who can do that equally well.' Nerienda was red in the face. 'I'm very sorry, Mother Abbess, but I'm not leaving until the last person has gone.'

'By which last person I suppose you mean Odel! Ridiculous, impudent girl – how can you say such things when we are all in danger? I am ordering you, as your Mother Superior, to take our sisters away from this place and lead them to safety. Now.'

'You cannot order me. I've been trying to tell you for days but you won't listen. I will never take my vows, never be a nun, here or in any community.' She tugged the veil from her hair, wrenched out the clips so her long black hair tumbled loose from its plait. 'From this day on, I renounce my position as novice.'

At this moment, the fire of sunrise flashed across the sky. Only, shockingly, it wasn't sunrise – the flashes were flames, distant but brilliant, streaking, gashing, overwhelming the whole horizon.

'Soham!' cried someone. 'It's Soham! The Abbey must be on fire!'

Suddenly there were other voices, people running and screaming, pounding on the church door, frantic to be let in.

'The king is dead!'

'They've murdered the king!'

'Shot him through with arrows like a hedgehog!'

'They're burning everything in their path. They're on their way here!'

'Ring the bells,' shouted Hilde. 'Ring the two bells.'

A score of people heaved on the ropes and the bells, clanging out, shook the ground under their feet, ringing out no celebratory peal but a dreadful, resounding tolling.

'The village!' Another cry. 'Our homes are on fire!'

And now the rest of the sky was scarlet, closer, spreading from farm to farm, building to building as the village burned.

'Run! All of you, run for your lives.' Hilde's voice was heard even above the screaming. 'Follow Odel, he knows the way to the secret paths. Odel, take them. Run! Keep them safe.'

'Mother,' Odel panted. 'My parents are there. In the village. My sisters! I've got to go back!'

'I'm coming with you,' cried Nerienda.

Hilde seized the frantic young man by the arm and pulled him close. 'Odel,' she whispered, 'there is nothing you can do to rescue your family now. They are in God's hands. You must save these poor souls here. I beg you. There is nothing else you can do.'

Odel, weeping, grabbed Nerienda's hand, running with her and the others who followed, running towards the woods.

~

There was an unnatural silence after the uproar. No screams, no sobbing, no tolling bell. Hilde walked slowly into the church and knelt at the shrine of the saint, marvelling at the beauty of the moment – a white cloth over the marble tomb, candles in every nook. Above her, golden angels were radiant in stained glass, the sky of scarlet fire outside making them shine.

She turned round quickly at a sound behind her. 'Godric,' she exclaimed. 'What are you doing here? I thought you had gone with the rest.'

'As if I would leave you.' He knelt down next to her. 'Whatever happens now, we shall face it together.'

'No!' Hilde stood up. 'Godric, you must run and catch up with the others. With Odel's knowledge of secret tracks there is a chance of escape.'

'I will not leave you, Mother Hilde. There's nothing more to say.'

'Yes there is! Are your writings safe in the cellar?'

He nodded. 'As safe as I can make them.'

'Then go on your way and be safe as well. One day you may return and take the parchments to a better place but now you must go. I have trusted you with my rambling tales and if you live, they will live on too. Hurry.'

She pushed him towards the back door of the church, shoved him outside. 'Go in safety. May God be with you.'

He looked at her, ready to plead. She slammed the wooden door shut, touched it gently with her hand. 'Goodbye, my dear son.'

A crash as a man came rushing in, axe swinging, stuffing silver and jewels into a sack, smashing a carving of the Virgin Mary, heading towards the shrine. His eyes were wild.

'You shall not touch this.' Hilde, her fists clenched, stood firmly in front of the tomb.

The man laughed mockingly, swung his axe at Hilde, felling her to the ground. With one swift move he heaved the cloth away, raised his axe again and smashed it down on the shrine.

The white marble cracked. A chip of it shot into the man's eye like a thorn. Screaming, he fell to the floor.

There was uproar as other soldiers burst into the church, snatching at ornaments, hurling statues at windows. Coloured glass shattered around the altar. Hilde, half conscious, thought she saw a white lily fall next to her, next to the man with the bleeding face who was lying in agony by her side. 'God will forgive you,' she murmured.

There were candle lights flickering on the altar, slowly growing dim. Hilde knew she should pray but the moment was fading, she was leaving the carnage, leaving the fear, going back, back – there was a song of exile and loneliness from a long time ago but there was love as well and a voice, a face. Hilde reached out slowly with her hand. 'Wulf,' she whispered. 'My Wulf.'

PART III

An early covering of snow added brightness to the March morning when I set out for a three day visit to Ely.

Research on foot – the best way. Imagination can scoot on ahead, sense ancient rain, the small bones in one's feet can start to touch base with fossils, sea-shells, Jurassic rock, forests of willow and oak. A way to feel beginnings.

For now, the surface of things was enough. Stuntney Causeway was thick with traffic but massive sheets of clear polythene were stretched over the green shoots that grew in the rich black soil, polythene that shone like the river that once came right up to the edge of Ely's Isle. At that time there were bustling, noisy docks where the lucrative trade in eels was conducted. Nerienda's father and brothers lived there. From Stuntney the girl was sent as a reluctant novice to Hilde's Abbey. Dissatisfied with her life, both present and past, she only re-visited the place once, in Godric's company.

Stuntney offered one of the few ways into the Isle. No one living there would have stood a chance as the Great Heathen Army, vicious on foot and on horse, plundered its way across the causeway, the flames of Soham Abbey red as blood behind them. Anyone left alive that day might have heard the Abbey's new Felix bell and its companion ringing out, too late, the sound of warning.

~

The marshes of Aldreth were another way that led into the Isle. They are drained and flatter now but still slippery and gleaming with puddles and mud. I wanted to follow in the steps of Hilde and her small group of nuns as they made their slow way to Willingham. Across this seemingly endless and bleak landscape, I walked as far as I could until driven back by weariness and ice in the wind. Hilde presented herself as full of confidence the day she went on her journey, boasting of her sure footedness, her knowledge of safe tracks across the swamp – but I think it would have been far more perilous than she was willing to admit, trudging through this tangled, waterlogged place fragmented by reed banks and fields of sedge.

That afternoon I found St Mary's in Willingham. There is a small, white room that most probably was once an anchorhold but it is a later medieval addition, not the dark, stone cell where my anchoress would have knelt, digging her grave in the dirt.

There was a surprise though; a gift. A series of wall paintings, whitewashed over for centuries, were revealed as faded and patchy but still with hints of colour and light. There was an extra joy: Etheldreda was here in an alcove, sketched on one side of a narrow window. Her sister, Seaxburh, was on the other. They had both survived.

Crows were cawing harshly at the back of the church 'Warning. Your presence has been detected and your movements are being recorded,' said a faint, disembodied voice behind the tall trees.

~

The sky above Ely Cathedral was blue and ducks wandered merrily on the grass outside as I continued my on-foot quest into Hilde's ninth century world.

East became West when the Great Ouse changed direction during the seventeenth century drainage of the fens. The river system around Ely is not what it was – a cause of confusion to amateur researchers like me.

Yet the geology is still intact in the underlying land mass and the layout of streets. Much, of course, now lies buried under modern housing estates, road junctions, traffic lights and a nearby aerodrome, but much has also been found by those who dig, sift and unearth. Saxon cemeteries around the city yield up skeletons, bits of pottery, brooches, glass beads of amber and blue. A gold cross pendant, believed to be a religious charm, made of crystal, garnet and amethyst has come to light. Could it have belonged to one of those royal abbess-princesses, Etheldreda's successors?

Archaeologists along West Fen Road have also discovered an extensive settlement that was probably part of the monastic estate before the Viking raid. There are traces of barley and wheat, the remains of sheep, cattle, poultry and pigs. Signs exist of vineyards and small orchards and there are hints of paths and plots of land. Odel's family may have lived somewhere in this space; Hilde would have walked down the hill from the abbey when she came to bring comfort and medicines to the sick father; the little sister may have found the crab she offered as a remedy for swollen eyes in the nearby river.

Springhead Lane is one of the oldest Saxon trackways. As I wandered along it at sunset there was something about the light that made me feel only a finger-tip touch away from sensing and learning more.

It was dark when I made my way back along the towpath, the river shining with lights from boats and bars. The pavement over the bridge was studded with lights as well, small moons guiding the way. There would have been no lights to guide the fugitives in my tale. Only the flicker of flame.

~

I wonder what Godric's thoughts would have been if he had received a vision of the future, or if, by some time-travel quirk of a parallel dimension, he found himself in this twenty-first century, wandering alone in present-day streets.

It is easy for us to re-create the past, or to imagine that we do. Battles are re-enacted bloodlessly, a TV series will inflict cockroaches and lice on actors who are paid to endure a week or two surviving a Dickensian slum. Smells are re-vitalised: we can sniff the stench of a gong boat or a blocked up Plantaganet sewer. Recipe books abound: we may cook ourselves a Tudor feast (minus the swan with a gilded beak) or we might taste a bowl of pottage and agree that the peasant had a healthy, if tedious, diet. There is no end to the stunning conclusions a forensic expert can reach – give one a skull, a box of bones, a tiny sample of DNA and in no time at all the shape of a woman or man will be re-cast in 3D, dressed mannequin-like in the clothes of the era and looking so realistic you might convince yourself it breathes.

What would we miss if we could go back, really go back to Saxon times? I for one would miss the comfort of a warm bed. I'd certainly feel the cold and the thought of spiders and rats lurking in the dark would make me shiver even more. Would I feel constrained by the lack of transport, miss my iPad and phone? Perhaps – but it would be hot water and shampoo that I'd yearn for most.

But for Godric, today, here and now. The world that he'd find himself in would seem fantastical. Terrifying, of course, with perils at every step. But if he somehow got used to the uproar, the huge mass of people, machines, discoveries, creations and staggering inventions, what sort of absence would tug at his heart; what would he be nostalgic for?

Firstly, I think, the stars, for there are fewer of them – or they are less visible now at any rate – and he'd wonder what had happened to all the birds, the sound of wing-beats in every tree and the incessant, melodious singing that Anglo-Saxon poets listened to and loved. And he'd be saddened by the creatures confused and out of their woodland settings – the road-kill of badger and hedgehog, the thin urban fox, starving and tipping up bins.

Above all he'd regret the loss of the air that had nourished him most of his life, not only the salty marshland tang or the odour of eels carried downwind, but the river smell; the green river smell.

And the light, so different now. Poor Godric, he would weep at the change; the shifting.

~

It's hard for a fiction writer to kill off his/her characters or leave them helpless in situations of danger and fear. Hard for a reader too. If I enjoy a book and the people in it have come to life for me, I want them to go on living in my mind, at least for a while.

Sadly, I need to leave Hilde felled to the ground by a Viking axe and dying on the altar steps as the Abbey's wooden rafters roared into flame and the stonework cracked, burst, blackened and crashed down around her. Her consolation in those last moments, I trust, will have been the memory of love.

That Viking who struck the shrine of the saint and was punished when the marble splintered his eye – can that have been Asmund? I have been imagining him as gentler, musing on fate, hoping his son would remember him for the honour of his name. I've pictured him playing his lyre around a camp fire at night, even composing the song "*I Dreamt Me A Dream.*" Foolish. There would have been no time for gentleness or for dreaming dreams in a raid.

I know I am holding back, unwilling to confront the fate of Odel, Nerienda and that scattering of nuns, monks and farmers who fled with them in terror. I hold out little hope of survival in the burning village for Odel's family – his father weakened by ill-health, his mother and sisters at the mercy of those who would plunder and rape. I wish all of them could have been saved or, at the very least, that the youngest child might have found a shelter to hide in or managed to fend off an attack with an eel greeve or farming shovel or was quick enough to drop to the ground and lie still as if already dead. Survival in the aftermath would have brought her trauma and loss – but I still like to think she lived.

And Odel? Where would he have gone? He knew the secret tracks and where small boats were hidden. The fugitives would, perhaps, have been safe in the forest for a while, living on whatever they could forage, hiding like foxes underground. But then where? The causeways at Stuntney, Earith or Aldreth again? Hilde had mentioned Peterborough as a possible sanctuary but accounts of the time describe ferocious scenes of fire and slaughter in East Anglia as the Great Heathen Army, heavy with plunder, seared its way from church to church.

Was anywhere safe? A historical map is marked with arrows of direction that show routes taken by the raiders. Almost every region is covered. Wessex held out and fought back but it was hardly a safe place to be.

Accounts of the time suggest that some while later eight members of Ely's community did return to the ruined site. So maybe Odel and Nerienda were among them. Did they creep home, trusting that since the land and church had been ravaged and stripped there was nothing else left to bring the raiders back? Maybe they found that a monk or two had managed to hide, or a few villagers had somehow survived, Odel's sister among them.

Imagination's reach is limitless but it's time to cry stop, leave what might have happened in the realm of enigma and allow the two lovers in this tale to find their own destinies, whether it be death in the marshes or a lifetime together sharing some moments of contentment and eventual peace of mind.

~

Enigma. A word whose etymology is as complex as its meanings. Latin *aenigma* translates as "riddle." From the Greek *ainigma* we get "a dark saying." After 1600 there is a slight shift in interpretation as enigma takes on the general sense of "anything inexplicable to an observer." We seem to be in the company of an unseen watcher now.

My definition of the word would include more than just the obscure and the complex. For me enigma is cloaked within the "dark saying." It is the riddle within the riddle; the space between the words.

Which leads me on to the Exeter Book with its store of puzzles which are enigmas in their own right.

This massive tone – *this mycel Englisc boc* – was bequeathed in 1072 to the library of Exeter Cathedral by Bishop Leofric. An eleventh century gifting but copied, experts suggest, by one scribe from various manuscripts or an anthology composed two or three centuries earlier. In this book – so heavy it may even have been used as a doorstop or a cutting board – are one hundred and thirty-one pages of narrative poems, wisdom pieces, elegies, charms, prayers and riddles. *Wulf and Eadwacer* is one of the texts.

So what obvious enigmas encircle the Exeter Book? First of all may be the issue of how it survived at all, reasonably intact – though with water marks, glue stains, knife cuts, fire damage and no original cover – for nearly a thousand years. This huge book has seen the Norman invasion, the Reformation, seventeenth century Civil War and, potentially most dangerous, World War II when the city of Exeter was heavily bombed.

Another puzzle is the layout: Modern theories tend to favour the idea that the volume is disordered and that somewhere along the way the booklets within it have been re-arranged. Expert opinion has analysed the parchments – all thin membranes with the writing on one side sometimes showing through to the other. But these membranes are of different grades: some are thick and rough with the texture of suede, the marks of the scraper revealed on both the hair and the flesh side. Other pages, however, are of better quality – thinner, smoother, the hair side more yellow, the flesh side white.

Leofric's gift is a literary treasure but a haphazard one – poems are interspersed with riddles, none of which have answers, the original pieces had no titles at all so it's often unclear where one text ends and another begins. *Wulf and Eadwacer* follows the poem *Deor* but then there is a block of sixty or so riddles before the next poem *The Wife's Lament*.

The hair side and the flesh side. Makes me think of the riddle Godric was muttering to himself as he wandered on the beach at Lindisfarne: *An enemy robbed me of my life, pillaged my strength, they plunged me in water, soaked me, then heaved me out and set me to dry in the sun.*

Or perhaps the pages are in the order they were meant to be – exactly the way the original anthology that was the precursor to the Exeter Book had set them out. There may be a very wide gulf between an Anglo-Saxon's idea of poetic order and ours.

Incidentally, there are eight original pages missing. They have been replaced. What was written on them? Where did they go? Are the new pages exact copies or is that another thing lost?

Godric. Could his be the hand behind some of the riddles and poems? Is it possible he escaped the monstrous attack and the fire that gutted the Abbey, fled to safety, returned at a later date to retrieve his manuscripts from the secret cell below the crypt, found his way to Italy or France, made himself known as a scholar and scribe, eventually came home? Certainly some of the riddles in the Exeter Book seem to be his – but maybe they were already well known. Again, there are parallels between Hilde's story and the unhappy woman in *Wulf and Eadwacer* – but perhaps this was a popular genre, a common theme with many variations on the tale.

And yet there is something about the Exeter Book in its entirety that makes me think of Godric. Is it the sense of wonder, a love of nature, a feeling that all things – animate and inanimate – are part of a living continuum and everything possesses its own voice? Throughout the texts there is an awareness of the transience of life, an acceptance of fate, a feeling of exile, an underlying sadness and a mood of loneliness – all qualities shared by Godric, that melancholy scribe.

One more detail. There is a riddle in the book about a cuckoo chick placed as an egg in an alien nest and nourished and reared by an unrelated mother. Was this Godric in his early days, his 'missing' years. Was he, like the cuckoo, hidden among strangers?

There are always alternative ways of looking. Riddles within riddles. Spaces and more spaces.

There are traces of gold leaf in the Exeter Book. In a past century thin sheets of leaf must have been pressed between the pages, the weight of the book used as a press. I like to think of those scatterings of gold gleaming in a ray of sunlight on an open page.

~

I feel I have been too dismissive of this story's saint. The more I read and think about Etheldreda, the more I realise how central a role she played, not only in the lives of my handful of characters, but in the whole history of Ely's Abbey lasting from that hour in the seventh century when, as princess, she was given Fenland acres as a marriage gift and founded the double monastery, right up to the dark days of the Reformation when Henry VIII's bully boys smashed her shrine to bits.

As the centuries passed, the myth of Etheldreda came to mean different things to different people. Bede saw her as a Virgin Mary for his time, an almost-Madonna to be cherished and idolised. Later, with the growth of Benedictine foundations, Etheldreda represented the purity and perfection of the monastic life. Her shrine in Hilde's lifetime must have shone like a thousand stars at midnight but later, with its cult status and a showering of wealth, it grew even more dazzling. At this later time as well, Etheldreda's reputation was enhanced by a cast of secondary characters, a support network of two of her sisters and a niece whose bones were dug up from their burial places and re-interred at Ely.

We have a description of effigies made of the four of them – Etheldreda, Seaxburh, Werburgh and Eormenhild – life-size, bejewelled, solid with gold and silver, placed two on each side of the high altar. What an impact they must have made.

The *Liber Eliensis* (History of the Isle of Ely) was written by an anonymous chronicler in the twelfth century. A large section of this is devoted to an account of the lives and miracles of Etheldreda and her sisters – a statement of strength to boost Ely at a time when it was suffering financially and in reputation.

I find it fascinating to see the transformation of Etheldreda into a warrior-like saint, a binding force to the monks of Ely who chose to side with Hereward the Wake and his rebels against William, the Norman ruler. Like an army with a rallying cry, these monks were proud to call themselves the Knights of St Etheldreda.

When it became apparent that they had chosen the losing side, the monks, and Etheldreda, quickly swopped their allegiance over to the king.

An anecdote about Etheldreda has stayed with me in the same way a nightmare can do. A Norman sheriff named Gervase tried to lay his hands on property belonging to the Abbey. The saint obviously saw this action as a personal attack on herself and promptly appeared to Gervase (her two sisters in tow) armed with a sharp staff. Challenging him for his contempt, she stabbed him close to his heart. Not to be outdone, the saintly Seaxburh and Werburgh came at him with their staves. Gervase made such an uproar as he screamed for mercy that members of his household came running. 'Can't you see,' he shouted (or words to that effect). 'Can't you see, in front of you, St Etheldreda and her sisters who have done me to death? And look – look – she is returning to kill me with a final blow.' At these words, the *Liber Eliensis* says, he breathed his last.

Truly the stuff of a feverish dream.

~

The *Liber Eliensis* compiled, it says, by a monk of Ely in the twelfth century, presents me with another enigma. I wonder if, like the Exeter Book, there are pages missing.

There are detailed accounts, for instance, of Etheldreda's role as Abbess until she died in 679 when she was succeeded by her sister, Seaxburh, who later handed on the duties to her daughter Eormenhild.

After the latter's death, her own daughter Werburgh took charge of the Abbey although she does not seem to have been around much in Ely, preferring to live in Staffordshire.

After 699 there is a gap, a jump in time, lasting over one hundred and fifty years, with only the briefest mention of "blessed women" whose names "are unknown to us." The next chapter details the arrival of the Vikings in 866 and the destruction, a few years later, of the Abbey.

Why are the names of these Abbesses unrecorded? Hilde would have been one of them. The *Liber Eliensis* painstakingly details all manner of incidentals. What has happened to the missing years 699 – 866?

A recently discovered document may hold some clues:

~

***Extract from a document claimed to be a section of manuscript from the twelfth century book the* Liber Eliensis:**

Well then, in these later years there were holy women in this place, though their names are now lost, who followed the path to Almighty God, as did the blessed Etheldreda and her sisters, those holy virgins of blessed memory. And many were the miracles recounted, for this place was made sacred by our glorious St Etheldreda who transformed the wilderness that had been stricken desolate by the pagan Penda, into a monastery where men and women might serve Our Father in Heaven according to the instructions set out by Saint Augustine whose name and memory are forever revered.

Now I have undertaken to unfold the history of these days and I beg that no man find fault with me, for not without effort have I learned of innumerable tales which I shall endeavour to relate.

But there is one tale the telling of which grieves me, for though the lady whose name is unremembered in the thoughts of men today - but whose holy deeds will not be forgotten by Almighty God to whom even the smallest sparrow that falls is counted and held dear - this most praiseworthy woman lived for many years as an Abbess in this place and many worthy kindnesses did she perform to the greater glory of God.

And the tale that is still told on the tongues of men must be an untruth for the devil knows well how to insinuate himself most craftily into the minds of men. For this untrustworthy tale recounts how the Abbess in her younger days, before she dedicated herself to the service of Almighty God – as did St Etheldreda of blessed memory – how in those days she found herself with child by one who was not her married lord and she did grieve and suffer greatly. But we must be ever mindful of the holy St Augustine himself who in his youth did live a most ungodly life for he was one who was persuaded by the wiles of Satan to follow the paths of wickedness until saved by the righteousness of Almighty God.

Now I have undertaken to speak only of the truth in these writings and to take no heed of idle talk and whisperings, for these events occurred a long time ago – many years before our blessed St Edmund was martyred most bloodily by the barbarians who, like the pagan Penda, despoiled this place – although our glorious St Etheldreda later recovered this monastery for the greater glory of God.

And so I will ease my aching wrist and write no more of this noble Abbess whose name is now unremembered, and I shall give no credence to foolish rumours that say she later sent for the child of this unholy union and had him live with her in this place and he, unknowing of the rumours and in ignorance of the kinship, lived as a holy monk beloved of Our Lord.

And if so, then let it be, for now this winding sequence must tell of other men and women who later on followed the path first begun by our glorious Saint whose memory shall never recede but be forever blessed...

~

So many are anonymous in this tale. The narrator of *Wulf and Eadwacer*, faceless artists, minstrels, scribes, nameless skulls and saints. All are hidden, compressed like fossils into anonymity. Our knowledge of the poet Cynewulf, for example, is a pittance. Godric may have come across him or his writings on one of his later travels and discovered more, but for us he is a drizzle of rain in the mist.

Pseudonymous

Cynewulf, the arc of the sun
swings more fiercely over this world
since you were here

We are reduced
to the thinnest of thin gold leaf
an ache
the length of the heart

A thin gold leaf – unlike
the rood, that shimmer in gold of your vision-tree –
oh the bliss, you cried, the bliss
of such a dream

which now shimmers
into distance
as even the best dreams do

and whatever that bloody tree learned in its life
creeps off
to a brown-rot mold

And of you, voice-bearer, what fibre is left?
Your name's an acrostic in a script
a tentative runic signature
nestled in text

Why this scarcely observable
gesture, this cryptic indication
you too were here?

Dream on, poor fellow –
we shall all be anonymous soon

~

It is now time to start embroidering the last threads on the cloth of this tale within a tale. I shall use some random anecdotes, most probably apocryphal, but pleasing ones for it is preferable to end, not with a ruined and desolate abbey, not with fugitives on the run, but on a merry note and with a tune.

An anecdote of reconciliation, perhaps, for it concerns Canute, a Viking king living about one hundred and fifty years after the fearful events of 869/870, ruling peacefully enough in the land his ancestors had ravaged.

Ely's Abbey Church was re-founded a century after its destruction. It became one of Canute's favourite places to visit and he would journey there once a year in February for the Feast of the Purification – the festival now known as Candlemas. Often his wife Emma would accompany him and we have an account of her gifting the Abbey with an altar cloth of green, red and gold and a covering of jewelled purple for Etheldreda's shrine.

February. An important month, then as now, midway between winter and spring, a time of growing and hope. *In this month*, states a calendar of the time, *begins the singing of birds*.

But early February is frequently cold and the Fenlands were frozen and thick with ice on the day Canute had planned to travel to Ely.

This ice, so says the account that has come down to us, stretched treacherously from Soham Mere to Ely and Canute was unwilling to trust his royal person to it. Luckily, a local man, a tough and well-built fellow, offered to lead the way, testing the ice with his weight. A delightful touch to the narrative tells us this man's name was Brithmer and his nickname Budde – which has been translated as Pudding.

And so the king, like Wenceslas' page, followed in his sledge as Brithmer skated ahead.

A tale that may have been true, or not, but it became famous and was passed on from father to son – as was another tale of Canute at Ely. This time he and his retinue journeyed by boat – for the river was close to the Abbey then, almost reaching the door. As they drew near the Abbey Church the sound of singing filled the air as the choristers of Ely raised their voices to celebrate the Feast. This song was written down in lyrics and musical notation three centuries after the day:

Merry sang the monks of Ely
As King Canute rowed thereby.
'Row boatmen, near the land,
And hear we these monks sing.'

And so, almost the final stitch in the cloth. It seems fitting we should leave lament and enigma behind as an early February sunset fills the vast fenland skies, winter ice shines for miles and the rebuilt church shimmers as a thousand white candles are lit for the Feast that began at one twilight and lasted to the next.

Sunset – yes – a fine time both to start and to end. A new day at the time of darkness; beginning.

~

Almost the final stitch in the cloth – but what about the beginning, the text of *Wulf and Eadwacer*, an enigmatic riddle-poem that like the tidal river on the Aldreth Marshes ebbs and flows and curves back on itself? Have Hilde's fragments muddied the pool of truth even more? Convoluted and ambiguous enough, the light footfall of one more earth-stepper will surely make little difference, add no more than a brief shimmer to the quality of light.

And maybe, after all, ambiguity is the whole point. Why else so many words with double meanings? Why else such paradox?

And I think it's correct, the theory that suggests one of the best ways to enjoy *Wulf and Eadwacer* is to read or hear it in the original. It may be all the years of arguments and translations that spoil the Anglo-Saxon beauty of the words. Listen to some of the readings on YouTube. Pauses and intonations, of course, are interpretations in themselves – but at least there is the magic of the sound. I have listened many times and been enchanted.

And possibly, at the end of it all, there is no single meaning, only loss and grief and a love that has nowhere to go.

Who knows? Best to leave it as an *image in water, that dead man walking who never lived.*

And yet – I love narrative and appreciate an ending to a tale that, if not totally happy, at least promises some hope. Wulf himself has personally said little in any of these anecdotes. It is his turn now to speak:

Wolf's Get

Begin with a riddle, my lord would say
those winter nights when I was his bard
and the mead-hall rang with my song:

'A harbinger of early spring
sometimes heard but seldom seen
I sing my name.

Abandoned by my closest kin
I bear the blast of others' scorn
the lightning-lash of rain.'

Now spear-men trap me in this fen
where flies with fretful-weary wings
lurk in a marsh-mire gloom.

Liars, all the ones who call me
outlaw, wolf's-get, thief:
they would kill my best of dreams
fell me at the forest's edge
allow the sea to sip my bone
clod me in dark earth.

I would have a sester of honey,
snout of a plough to furrow my land
the fins of an anchor to hold me steady
in the dash and dazzle of waves.

Wait, my girl with plaited hair,
wait at dawn by Cyrtlan gate,
the deer pool next to Tuha's tree,
wait three days for me.

The cuckoo is the bird of spring
who cries his name in double notes
and warms his frost-breath winter quills
with candles of the sun...

Now let Spring,
that laughter-smith, bind
the eagle's claws in blossom,
fill a basket with blue sky and tip it
down through heaven's leaves to drench
my roots, to sing, to bring me home.

Mandy Pannett works freelance as a creative writing tutor. She has won prizes and been placed in several international competitions. She has also acted as adjudicator for other competitions and has edited publications by Sentinel Literary Quarterly and Earlyworks Press.

Other published works by Mandy Pannett include:

Poetry

'Bee Purple' – Oversteps Books
'Frost Hollow' – Oversteps Books
'All the Invisibles' – SPM Publications
'Jongleur in the Courtyard' – Indigo Dreams Press
'Ladders of Glass' (English Romanian parallel texts) – Integral Contemporary Literature Press

Fiction

'The Onion Stone' – Pewter Rose Press